ALSO BY MARK Z. DANIELEWSKI

House of Leaves

Only Revolutions

The
Fifty
Year
Sword

Mark Z. Danielewski's

The
Fifty
Year
Sword

by

 Pantheon Books New York

The Fifty Year Sword

Pantheon Books and colophon are registered trademarks of Random House, Inc.

Library of Congress Cataloging-in-Publication Data

Danielewski, Mark Z.
The fifty year sword / Mark Z. Danielewski.
p. cm.
ISBN 978-0-307-90772-1 (hardback)
1. Children—Fiction. 2. Revenge—Fiction.
3. Texas, East—Fiction. I. Title.
PS3554.A5596F54 2012   813'.54—dc23   2012010372

Printed in China

 . . .

First American Edition

2 4 6 8 9 7 5 3 1

Pantones:
1675 U, 124 U, 021 U, 186 U & 483 U
(Orphans). 287 U, 146 U, 356 U &
2602 U (Homes, Lovers & Others).

Fonts:
Dante (Title), Apollo (©, etc.),
Legacy (Dedication, Handle & Blade)
& Gilgamesh (Credits).

www.markzdanielewski.com
www.pantheonbooks.com

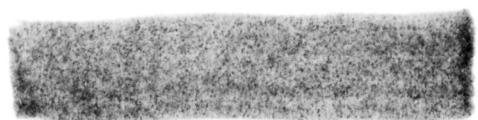

For

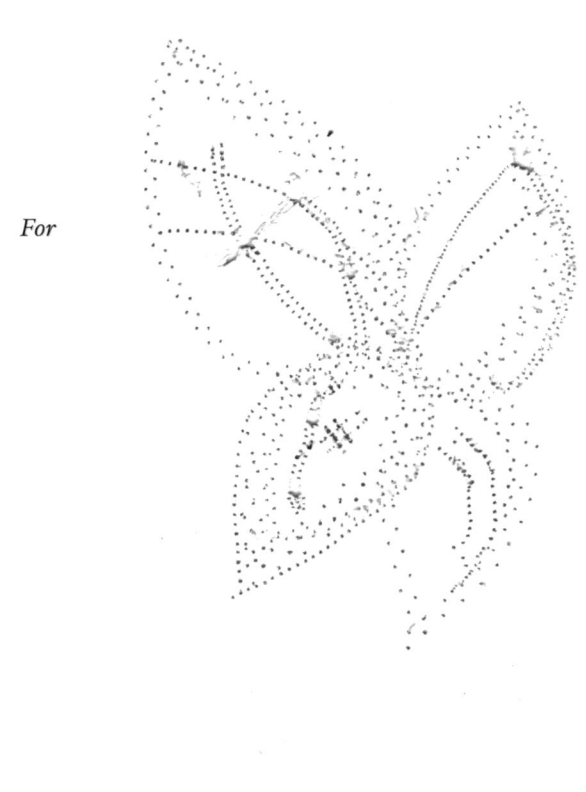

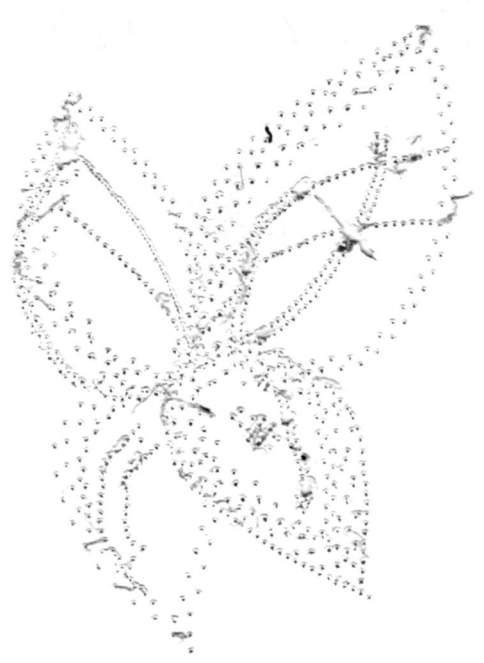

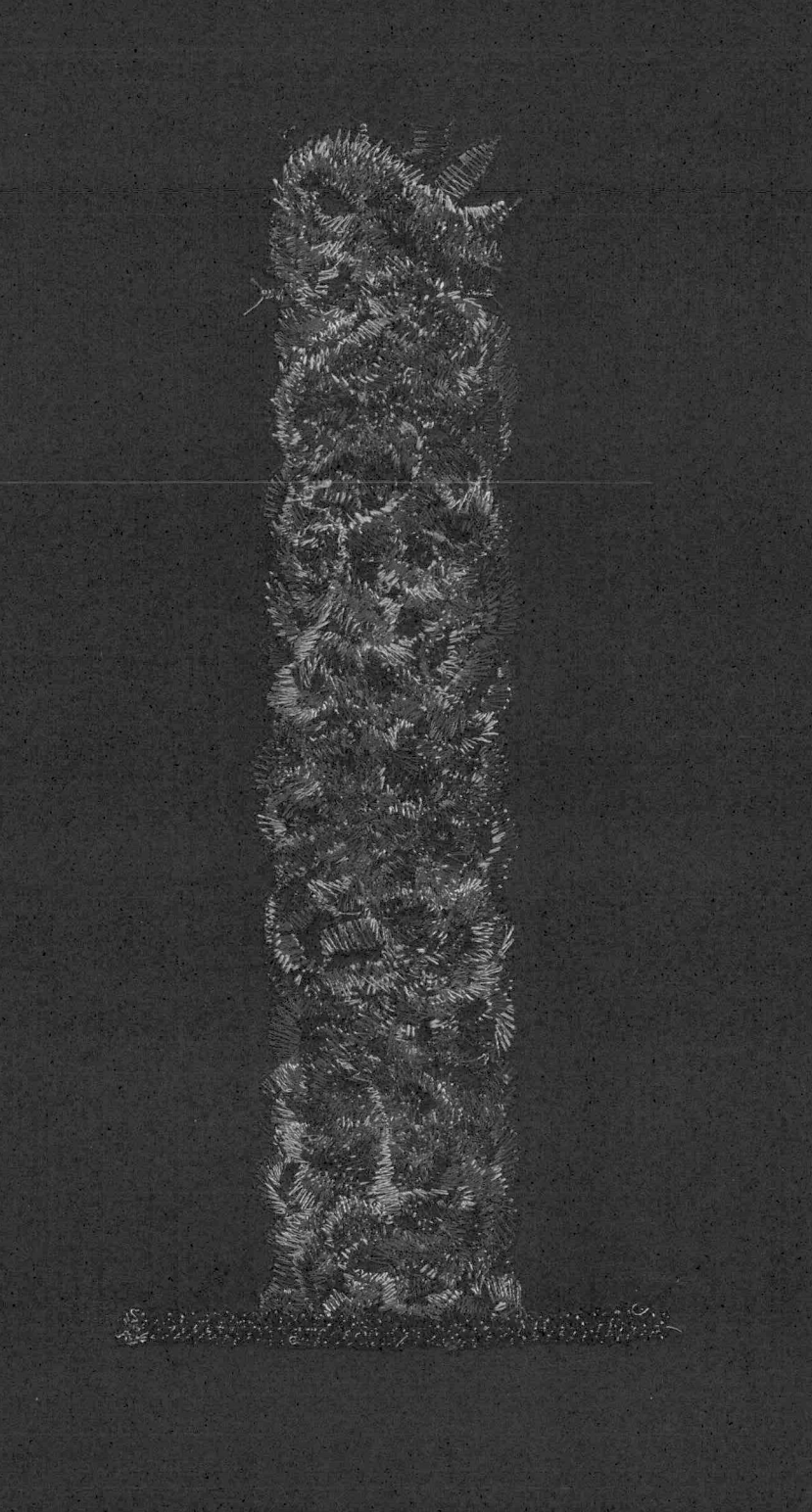

*Maybe because
the history of any ghost story
is a ghost story unto itself,
which is to say another story
completely, assuming any
of what follows can rightly
even be considered a ghost
story; rather than delve into
the devices and biases and
oddly canted idiom of the
five persons—one of whom
in the early years slept with
another and now endlessly
wonders about the lakes of
fall where someone else once
wandered; two of whom
still nurture their affection
for one another, expressing
so in an array of notes and
overseas phone calls; a fourth
who lost three; and the last of
whom from the prison of a
later life hates them all—or
represent them throughout
with characterizing phrases,
temporal references, and
even more quotation marks
hopelessly nested within
reiterating nests of still
more marks; to delineate
their respective and
independently conducted
interviews, colored quotation
marks are used instead:
" = 1, " = 2, " = 3, " = 4, " = 5.
Where no quotations appear
only the worst should be
assumed: an interruption
by someone other than one
of the before mentioned
persons, the reader or even
the author who additionally,
it must be stated, has done
nothing more than lend
together these gathered
and rerelated bits so as
to here present a pretty peculiar and perhaps altogether
alternate history of one October evening in East Texas. —MD*

"No matter how you cut it,

                             "no
matter,

        "Chintana near didn't accept.
"Only at the last moment, for reasons
vague,

        "if vaguely professional,

                           "did
she force from herself a reply, in the
affirmative, obviously, to

                      "accepatate,
"yes, accept

        "the invitation,

                        "Mose
Dettledown's invitation.

"Fact is, what Chintana had discovered since the divorce was that most everything required

                              "Force!

"Opening her eyes, her hands, even opening her medicine cabinet.

                              "Forced!

"Force open the can of bitter tea leaves. Force back the tough tongues of those walking shoes she kept perched "by a birdcage.

"Force even a smirk she hoped could serve, temporarely at least, as a not so scored and hearthunted a

                              "shimile.

"Especially when in the acknowledgement of something she recognized as Social Duty she was forced to acknowledge,
                    "yet again,
                              "to yet
another insitrusive customer,
her husband Pravat's surprising departure.

"Hmmmm, Pravat.

"Pravat.

.

"Force back something else too,

                                     "mustn't
forget that—

            "the terrible agony she
wished day out and night in to lash
across the throat of anyone who forced
from her all such incessant acts of
acknowledging
                "in the first place.

"Despite pacific beliefs,

only infliction

promised her

peace.

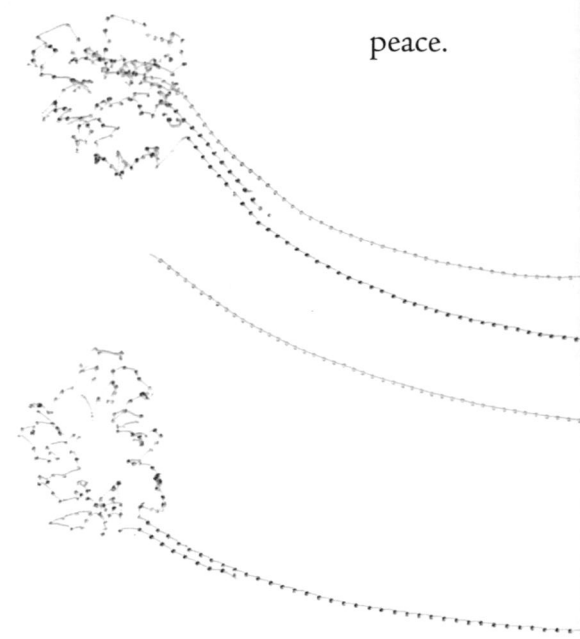

"And for sure,

              "as Chintana had
found out,

              "what came most effortlessly
to her nowadays had already happed

                         "but
five weeks earlier when the scissors, doing
their happy skew across the

                  "bias of a
Patent Lawyer's drapes, dancing silvery
"sharp through the separating cotton,
arrested finally when their metal V
wedged deep into her

              "soft thumb.

"She lost the nail but the local
Hand Surgeon had stitched back the
flap.

      "Taped on a butterfly for good
measure too.

"And she had forced herself to thank
him and,

        "somehow,

           "carry on.

"But she did not then as she could
not now seem to acknowledge to herself
just how easily she could have

                "seen it
happ to someone

         "else

            " 's thumb.

"And so of course
                    "Chintana had
once more reconsiderated
                          "whether or
not
      "she'd make it
                    "to Mose Dettledown's
Halloween party.

      "And seems she probely would have
taken a miss had it not been for her twin
"stitchimicated
                    "in Austin
                              "who had
sternly counseled—

            " 'Risk it.'

      "So Chintana had risked it, preparing
her bitter tea and swallowing hard before
leaving behind the thread and machines
of her trade,
                    "her unoccupied cage,
"Alba to Quitman on 182 East
                              "driving its
stabbing hope through the fallen dark.

"Chintana always found the
praticulars of Mose Dettledown's
gatherings odd
                    "but what else could one
expect from a 112-year-old nut job still at

ease

      "in those detirating ribs of her East
Texas remove slunk down amidst the
hickory
        "and Mexican wild
                "plum?

    "A few times a year Mose would
generously serve up booze
                "and sweet
"to fortipify the many strangers against
the expected strangeness of her minglings,
where someone like Chintana, a seamstress,
could find herself
           "deflecting the
advances of an inebriated City Alderman.

  "Mose though rarely appeared
herself. In fact running into her at all,
certainly tonight, would be like crossing
up with a ghost.

    "Though a ghost would be nice.

    "Crossing up with a ghost, thought
Chintana, was about the only thing that
would keep her from cutting her own
appearance short.

  " In fact Chintana had only gotten as
far as the coat rack when she thought for
the third
        "and last time
            "about retreating.

"This being so because the very first person
          "—not the third or even the
"second but the very
                    "first person—
"she was forced to smile at was the already smirking Belinda Kite.

    "Belinda!

    "Right there in Mose Dettledown's foyer atrium,
               "Belinda Kite eyeing Chintana's entrance with shearing scrutiny,
          "more redeyed than a coyote sniffing a saltblock in drought
"banglerattle arm twisting rattler mean into her side,
               "gums receding around the dead shine of her teeth like—

    " 'Well now if it isn't Mzzz Lost and Let Down,'

               "Belinda Kite might have snipped.
          "Or more benignly—

    " 'Deliveries in back.'

    "Or just a lucky carnal cluckity click.

"And maybe something like so did actually tickle her teethtickling lips.

                              "But it never got no further,

                    "not that night,
"and what a cold, cold night it had already become,

                    "because

                              "the sharpest tongue in East Texas knew better. One word, even the slightest indacitation of intimacy could very well have brought about her own

                    "extinction.

    "And

              "Oh!

          "had the two women actually touched,
              "a pat perhaps,

              "Oh!

                    "something slight and passing,

              "Oh!

"the results would have been cataclysmic, even worse

              "—unimaginable.

"And so right there on the spot,
"those pocketed eyes
                    "flittering nervously
around like a murder
                    "of crows told
Chintana
            "Belinda Kite knew exactly
what she had become.

"Here then was another consecawence
of Belinda Kite's stolen times with
Pravat.

"Belinda Kite who could routinely
make anyone cry from Fort Worth to
Nacogdoches,
                "who most certainly
would make some poor wretch cry
tonight,
            "saw right then
                        "right there
"right square in the middle of Mose
Dettledown's foyer atrium something
she could not challenge,
                        "or even
reach for,
            "and so pratically ran,
"scurrying backwards, pocketed eyes
flying off to a side
                        "until all of her was
sidewinding gone for the stammer of
guests in the back.

" Chintana shook and sighed and reconsidered her twin's counsel. "Maybe some things aren't worth the risk.

"And then along came the little ones.

"And that sure put a change in her.

"After all, what did they
"know
about risk?
"Or care for that matter?

"They
"were too young. Their play,
"the privacy of that pratical mayhem and racket,
"protected them. Zigzagging this way, there
"way, dashdown diversion fast across a dining room,

"eastern cottontails!

"sweet baby bobwhites!

"down some stairs, spinning sideways, socks slipping them up some
"on the smoothgrooved floors,
"but those small hands always grabbing fast enough,

"opossum grip for a corner!

"just in time to catch the slide and swing them in a celerating arc towards another warped hall.

   "And sure, sure come spring the wraparound porch outside with its gape at the sweet gum,
                    "loblolly pine
                                        "and
maple, could serve their turns,

   "preniscent turns,

                    "but tonight
"with a wind already whipping up something wrong,

                    "the dogs howling
in their kennels,

                "five such
                            "orphans
confined their tie-dye hues to the shadow of adult conversation and back rooms
"steeped in abandonment.

   "Theirs was abandonment's insurrection.

                "The coop de grass of feral play.

   "And so they flung themselves so,
"panting and rosy, past the foyer door

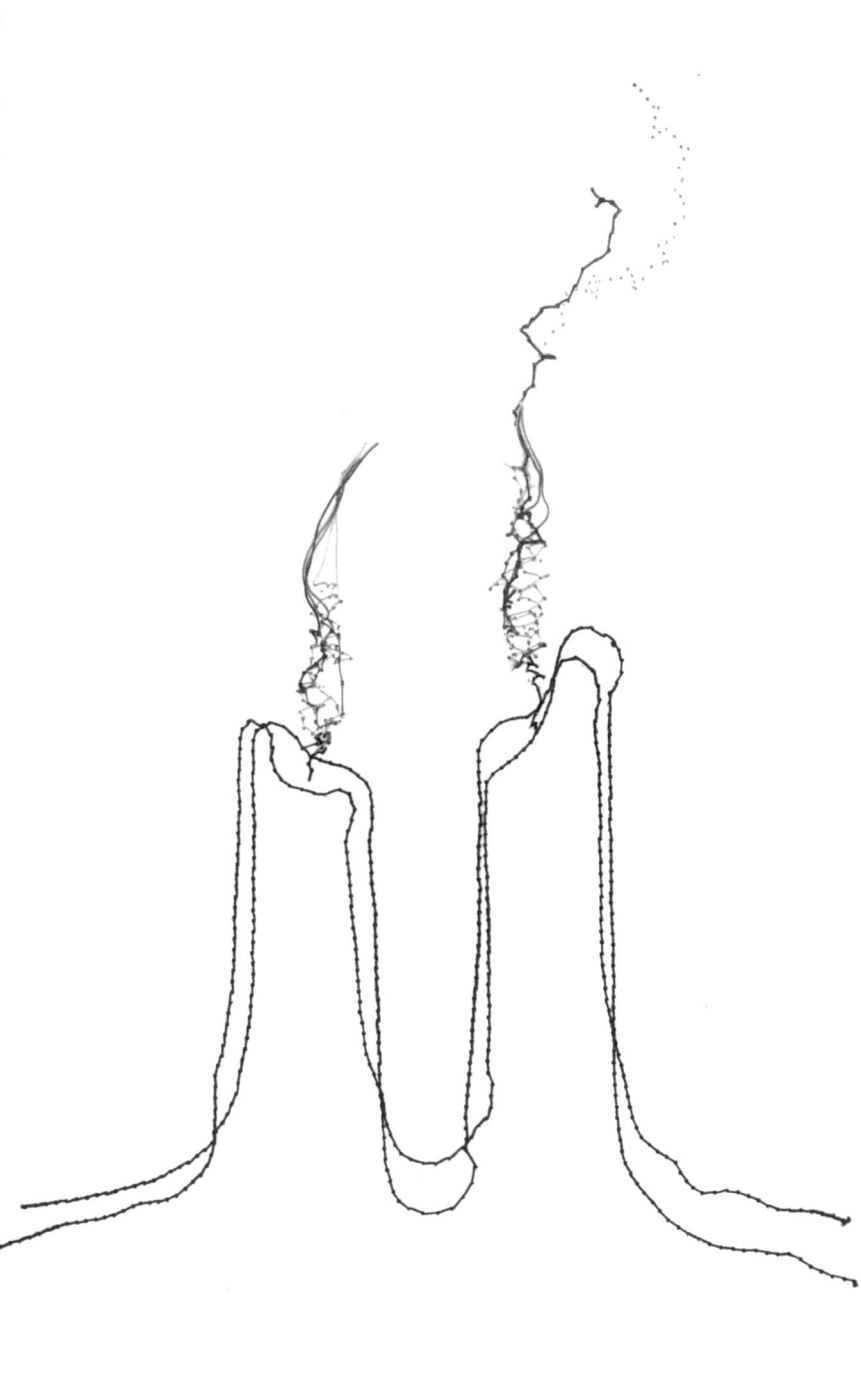

"astride their steeds—sticks palomino,
buckskin,
           "sorrel, bay and black, and
"Chintana felt herself warm and ease.

    "Here was enough.
    "They were enough.

    "And even if Chintana wasn't quite
able to put her thumb on it, how strange
still that just five
                "orphans,
                           "with but
the patpitter of their footsteps,
                           "on such
an instance,
           "after such an incident,
"could catchstitch, a bit at least, the
lacerations of grief six months continued
to inflict. Their offer somehow different
from everything else.

    "Something mock felled and clean.

    "As if to say,
                "so to say
                           "or so it seemed

        "—there was time.

                    "There was time.

    "Yes, there still was time.

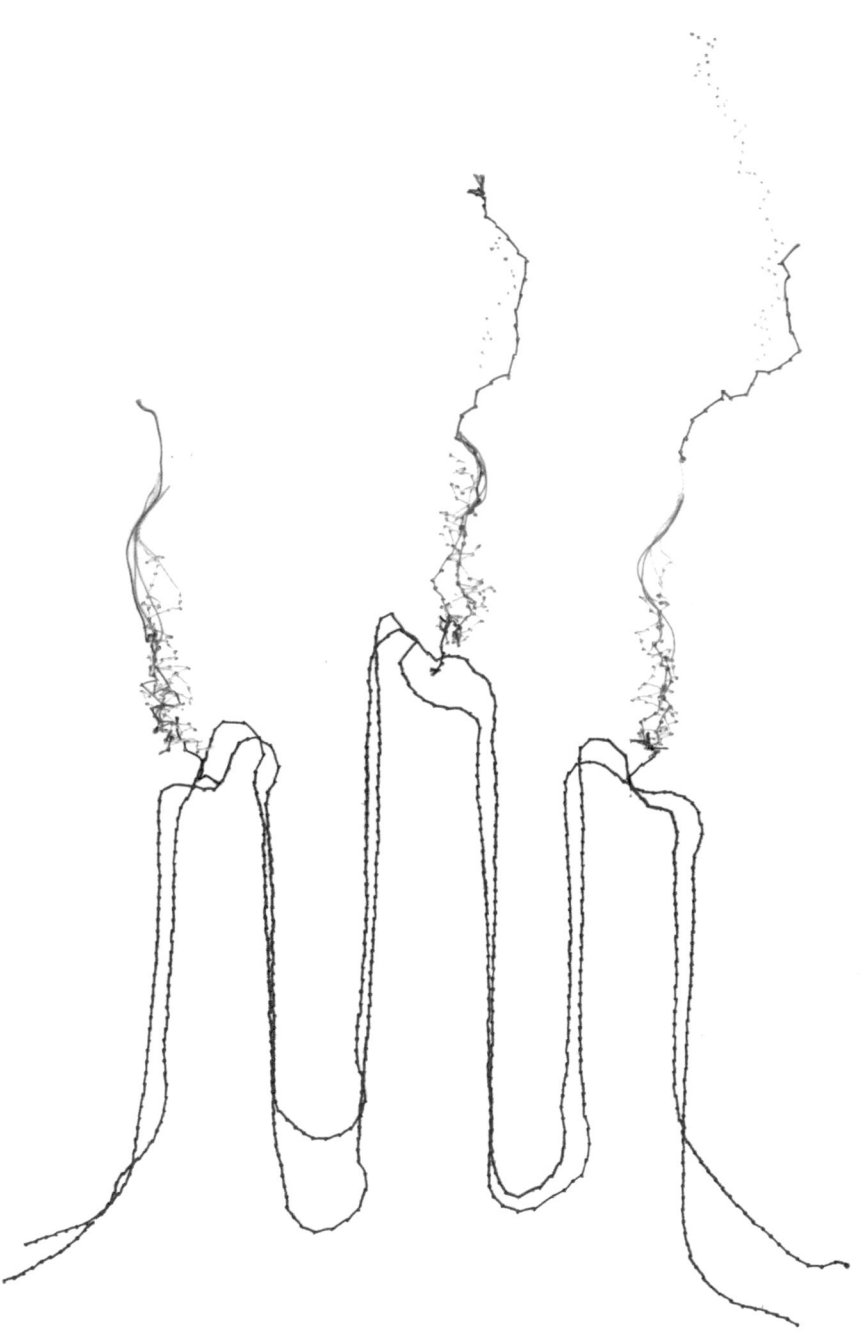

"So maybe Chintana had misconstrued Mose Dettledown's invitation after all—

"*Wallops of Scotch Dear. Don't deprive yourself of the Pleasures of my Company. Or my good Chear.*

"Maybe Mose hadn't been insitinuating matching pleasures with a local Stone Cutter
                    "or Silo Manufacturer.
"Or for that matter saber rattling with the likes of Belinda Kite.
    "Maybe Mose had only implisighed the pleasure of
                    "these five.

"So Chintana shed her grave coat along with the cold still slicing across the fields,
            "down through the fallen redbud and trumpet creeper,
                    "and fast enough found herself chatting with the Social Worker trailing the stampede,
 "where she learned that this year Dettledown's Halloween would end "at mindight with
                    "'someone's birthday.'

"'Whose?' Chintana wondering, "stuffing her wool scarf into her coat sleeve.

" 'Stitch in my side if I know,'
shrugged the sleepy Social Worker.
'My tired feet.'
    " 'They're a handful.'
    " 'Oh sweetie if only I could get my
hands on them to say.'

    "Chintana offered to find coffee and
when the Social Worker's eyes responded
"quicklit bobcat bright with a yes
                        "Chintana
happily headed off, threading her way
through the crowd and the ever helter
of severed mutters—

        "—'—Mightier than, and
unkindest of all—'

            "—'—Dull though—'

    "—'—Of course I mean the Dam!—'

                    "—'—Ask us!—'

"—parrying on the way a lutching Bob
Sandlin Park Ranger and even an
                            "I-
Wanna-Cut-Up-A-Rug-With-You Gas
Station Owner,
            "swaying on fumes while
wheezing about tax cuts and that 'Damn
Oak Lease'

"until she was—

"—'—in time saves nine—'

"—'—to the
quick—'

"—'—nickety nick nick—'

"—'—real *tranche de la vie*, her—'

"—edging in on tankards of steaming
beanbrew and cider, where Chintana
overheard from a
                    "Car Dealer
                              "and
"Taxidermist that the birthday in
question
           "was a champagne birthday,
"and a fiftieth birthday no less—

    "—'Not surprised she was carved
out at midnight,' one said.

        " —'She insists to the second,'
said the other.

        "—for none other than
                              "'that
bitchwitch Belinda Kite.'

" Chintana all too gladly retreated
"to the quieter reaches and vacancies
of the ranch,
                "her cupped take sloshing
in hand,
                "mind made up to leave long
before midnight,
                "refinding at last the
orphans dricketing on
                "furniture and
walls like so many mad, mad pileated
woodpeckers,
                "beaver busy.

        " 'Too many hours,' shoomed the
Social Worker,
                "gratefully accepatating
Chintana's concotions.
        " 'Don't know how much longer I can
do this. I've my own kids too, to keep
after, so, but, I guess these also are—'
        " 'Worth the extra coffee and sugar?'
Chintana finished.
        " 'I imagine they are the sugar.'

        "And right then a
                "young boy,
"frenzied as a storm-startled wood
squirrel,
                "dashed over— 'Can we stay for
the party?'
        " 'If we did Tarff, you would have
to sit with the adults and talk with the
adults and act like an adult. No fidgets

|44|

or fusses. Not one peep.'

"And that sure made nine-year-old Tarff
fidget plenty.

"Which hardly curtailed
the four-year-old girl's

"cottontail
curiosities:

"—'But what about the supwise?'

"'Ezade, Iniedia, Sithiss,' the Social
Worker called out to the two eight-year-
olds

"and seven-year-old

"in mid-raccoon
frolic,

"cutting decks, scattering decks, of
long ago

"ravaged cards.

"'Our Micit,'
the Social Worker continued, 'has asked
about the surprise. But I'm only going to
say this once.'

"And so the orphans rerounded,
collided,

"a sudden blue jay avirarity
wheeling as one, before finally settling
on the fence of quiet attention.

"'Yes, Mose Dettledown has arranged
a surprise,

"'a special surprise for you
and the other

" 'youngens
" 'this night.
But weather seems playing for some
delay here, so we'll need to show some
" 'patience.
" 'Until then, there is the
matter of some cake.'

"Whereupon,
"and near instantly too,
"Chintana was lost in the swirl and riot
of squeals and shouts until just as
"suddenly,
"they were gone—

"Tarff,

"Ezade,

"Iniedia,

"Sithis and

"ittle Micit,

"—five white-tailed deer in race,
       "fleetly
bounding by and around the knees of
minglers and newcomers,
       "racing
slickswitch quick down long halls, far,
far and away,

     "whippoorwills!

    "cedar waxwings on air!

"straight at last for those far away
kitchen doors battering out
       "large slices
of buttery light.

 "'Could lose a hand,' Chintana
laughed.
 "'Could lose more than that,' the
Social Worker gleamed.

 "'What sort of surprise is it this year
anyway?'
    "And the Social Worker, already
trudging after the orphans, shrugged—

 "'Just a

    "'Story

       "'Teller.'

"Breath, gentleness and gratitude, Chintana's twin typically counseled, "must precede Love.

"She was a Yoga-body, meditating, low-carb,

"Tibet-trekking, cat-lover.

"And a butcher to boot.

"'That's why before any heartstuff,' "—voice happily prickstitching the shifting

"cellular

"connection—

"'you first breathe and thank. And practice breathing and thanking. And gently too. With every breath.'

"Chintana had tried to practice. But just breathing required so much force it was almost inconceivable to imagine gratitude.

"Let alone gentleness.

"And anyway, gratitude for what or who?

"What about Belinda Kite?

"Belinda Kite?

"Belinda Kite!

"The idea rushed spouts of color
to her face. That lavish creature of
bleach and gold? Proudly pedigreed in
the bloodlines of Texas bullery with a
predatory,
                    "if curstatory taste,
                                        "for
minor men of all sports,
                                "usually not
citizens neither,
                        "offering the poor
minority the charity of her shape
and touch?
                    "Offering them their reverie?
"Who would as casually buy a Mercedes
as dole out mercy every other year? Her
mercy last year in the back seat of her SUV
with one of those boat people,
                                "a Thai
flowerman married to a
                            "Thai seamstress,
"a tight muddy man who could tenderly
lift fields of Wild Lupine,
                            "Blackberry
Lily
    "and lush Evening Primrose from
the grieving earth.

    "Neither Chintana nor the marriage
could afford that kind of Mercedes
                                        "or
survive that kind of mercy.

"Pravat never had a chance. And the loss of some larger dream for him,
"some
cultural intratwining,
"colilusion,
"coupled
with the betrayal, Belinda Kite's and his own, left him too cut up inside, all so gutted and gutless after all,
"to carry on.

"And to have him,
"all Belinda had had to do was press into his cupped hands a frail bit of embroidery her own fingers had
"clumsily threaded, and at points
"bled upon,
"barely managing with crewel white work and a forbidden stitch the
"smocking shade of a single

"Harvester
"with dark orange
"wings.

"To leave him though,
"and soon after too,
"Belinda Kite was far more bloodless—

"a pasty blue-eyed ex-officer
explaining in diligent tones how even
stepping towards a doorbell could be
read as trespassing
                    " 'and so punshable
by the law.'

    "Chintana found out every disconcerting
detail, and even,

                                "snip snip,

                "undid,

        "clip clip,

                                "stitch by
stitch,

            "the offending thief,

                                "intoxicant!

            "spell-casting lure,

"because Chintana had been the only
one Pravat knew well enough to confess
his torture to.

"When he left in April,
                            "flights of
green-backed herons shrieking in his
brow told her
                    "what he'd already made
of his wife but the
                        "falling egret
                                    "on his
lips also told her
                    "he had finally stopped
bleeding inside.
                        "He could smile vaguely
again,
        "limply clap her hand with his
two riverbed hands, nodding gratefully
only because like the desiccated rows of
his flowers and tears,
                        "black cratches, all
of it now,
            "mere shadows on the grey,
"he too like a passing day
                            "was already
gone.

" The Social Worker had mentioned
other
        "youngens
                    "but that night
Chintana saw no sign of any more.
    "Maybe the incresiating cold
                            "or the

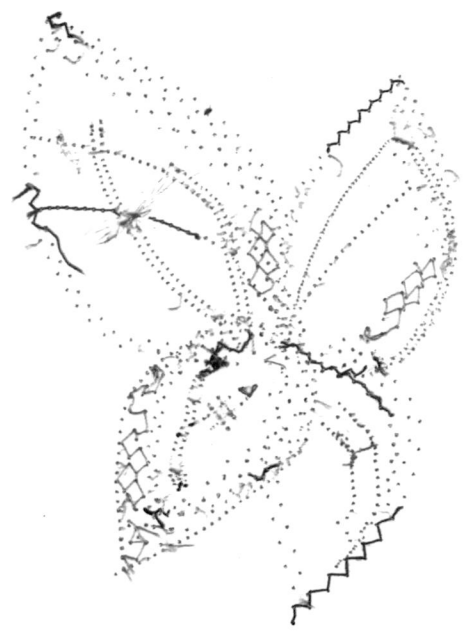

peculiar threat of a storm
                         "or Belinda
Kite's birthday
                    "had turned parents
from wrestling with seat belts and car
seats—
            "—from those oh so
                              "many lists
of babysitters tacked conveniently by a
phone.

    "Chintana rubbed the violet line
on her thumb as a woman with topaz
clamped on her ears burst past her
towards a small bathroom tucked
under the main stairs.

    " 'Such a hateful whore,' the woman
sputstuttersobbed to Chintana,
                              "to no one
in particular,
               "diving for the comforts of
lock and running water.

    "Whereupon Chintana's thumb
abruptly began to sore a little
                         "and she
felt bleak,
            "as if a thousand
                         "vengeances
upon vengeances were dicing her
suddenly
          "into hail.

"Though the cause was none too mysterious
            "—the front door just stood wide open.
            "Though when it had been flung so Chintana would never remember.

    "The porch lights were extinguished too, oddly,
            "and what's more a shadow now cut across the threshold,
                    "though without moon or stars in the Texas sky this was an awful impossibility,
                            "for here reaching towards her it seemed was a shadow cast by nothing
                    "other
                            "than the darkness itself.

    "Most would've denied the sight with a turn,
            "a cry,
                    "flight,
"but maybe because Chintana too, day out and night in, could so easily consider doing the same,
            "what would leave these rooms drenched in silence,
                    "and blood,
"she welcomed him.

" 'The orphans,'

   "was all he said.

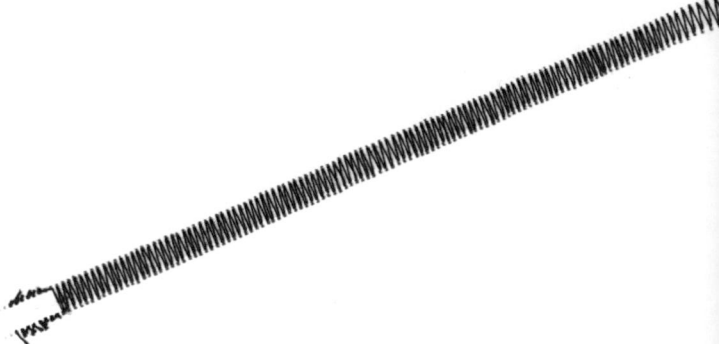

   "And Chintana showed him the way.

❝At first the five
                    "orphans,
                                    "five jittery
swamp rabbits,
                    "five knowsomebetter
gophers,
            "recoiled at the sight of
                                    "the
Story
        "Teller.

   "It didn't help that the library had not
suited his tastes, so his hulking form,
                                    "bent
and growling,
            "had led them up a
tightwind of back stairs into a small
parlor already dimly lit with
                            "five season-
poured candles of ginger,

                        "cinnamon,

"nutmeg,

            "cloves

                        "and molasses,

"clustered in an uneven arc away from
five dark windows, all tightly closed.

   "(Surely Mose's work.)

"Only when he finally sat down on
the floor did the orphans seem to relax,
"enchanted quick enough by the manner
of his diminishiding,
                              "so crossing his legs,
folding himself into himself,
                                    "refolding,
until right before their eyes he no longer
seemed
          "hrowling or gulking but sat
quietstill,
              "overdraped in his strange
silveryblack tunic, his head heavily
bowed.
    "Following this example Tarff, Ezade,
Iniedia, Sithiss and Micit sat down too,
"crossing their legs, and if not
                                    "exatecly
little
        "and bushy-bluestem cozy
                                    "then
armadillo tight,
                  "wanting now only to
know what was

              "—inside.

    "As for the Social Worker, with
her burden of watchful responsibility
momenterarily suspended,
                              "she took her
place in a back corner lounge chair and
"stretching out her legs,
                              "yawned.

"Chintana as well succumbed to her own shadows and seat,

                "trying idly to figure out

         "this figure's peculiar origins,
"the narrow eyes or sharp squeezed brows,

       "the profoundly wide forehead
"or the dark lips rounding out into the deeper creases of his cheek,

              "all mute and formless but somehow adding up to something Chintana knew only as

    "—awfully.

"Or perhaps it wasn't him at all but another question of origin—

       "the box he carried.

"A narrow thing with angles of black,
"six feet long, easy, with an ochre sash for a handle above the odd engraving—

    "T50YS

"The four hinges faced in towards him. The five metal latches faced out towards the orphans.

       "The number of latches confused her and warned her
"but Chintana didn't know what to do with warnings anymore.

"'What I have to tell you,'
"he began
slowly.
"'I must show you. But what I
show you I must also tell you. I have only
myself and where I've been and what I
found and what I now bring.
"'And it will frighten you.'

"This was not the way such
"tales for
five
"such orphans
"usually began.

"Micit cocked her head to one side
and Ezade's hands fussed in his pocket.

"Well maybe there would still be some
fun, Chintana mused.
"Maybe the Story
"Teller's strange and pompous gravity
would be refused with
"fitterings and
"frowns.

"Yet if the cloudy phrases released
them, his ever so slight nod towards the
box recaptured them.

"'All I have to offer is right here to
see, but if you scare easily you should
leave.'

"Tarff looked at Ezade
                    "who looked
at Iniedia who looked at Sithiss
                              "who
looked at Micit who defiantly looked
back at the dark
                    "man and his
                              "long
box
      "with angles of black
                    "and so they
all stayed.

      "'I am a bad man with a very black
heart. And it was only that badness and
blackness which forced me to seek out
what I have
            "'carried now for many
years and brought this night for you.
      "'Because you are young I will tell you
I went in search of a weapon.
                        "'But also
because you are young I will not tell you
why I went in search of such a weapon,
though in truth while I could speculate,
"'I am no longer capable of recalling the
details myself.
            "'When you are older you
will be able to imagine what drove me on
such a
      "'quest.
                  "'You will know then
more than me.'

"But saying this he did not look at the orphans, only at Chintana.
                    "And maybe it was a coincidence but her thumb began to hurt a little more.

      "'At first I went to places I knew.
"'Familiar places.
                    "'I examined ropes and knives of many sorts.
                          "'I considered oils and poisons.
                    "'I toyed with explosives.
                "'I handled guns. Small guns, big guns, guns powerful enough to
                                      "'sever something,
                "'anything, in half with just one blast.'

      "Chintana shifted uncomfortably.

"Where were the animals,
                          "the gleefully abandoned, or
                    "the stormy skies appropripriate for a
                          "ghost story for the young?

      "Where was the comedy?

"The Social Worker, however, seemed unconcerned.
            "That or too exhausted to resist the comforts of her recliner.

    "'But none of it,' the Story
                    "Teller continued,
            "'could match my taste for what my blackness ceaselessly scratched for.
    "'And so I traveled farther and farther away.
        "'From North to
                    "'South, Mountain to
    "'Valley, Coast to
                "'Coast.
                        "'Season by
    "'Season.
            "'Until finally I left the country on a ship, setting out for away and far places where faces are different
    "'and songs cradle words neither you nor I have ever heard.
    "'And everywhere I stopped, everywhere I ate,
                "'or drank,
                        "'or slept,
    "'I asked about
            "'a weapon.

"'Yet even in those distant places I received the same response—

"'ropes, knives, poisons, explosives and guns.

"'I shook my head and my heart blackened more and my badness spread so that

"'whatever I touched, my badness touched too

"'and seeped into.

"'Until finally one night on the banks of a muddy flow,

"'what some might call a stream,

"'on the edge of another dirty city,

"'I took cover from a rain beneath slabs of concrete twisted through with rusted rebar and

"'pain. It was a shelter I soon discovered already populated

"'by rats

"'but where I also overheard a story about

"'a valley assault and

"'a forest of note

"'and a mountain of

"'any

"'won

"'paths and a man with no

"'harms who made terrible weapons which he sold but never for

"'money.

" 'Intrigued I asked for a retelling of
the story.
" 'Carefully then I listened,
" 'memorizing every detail, prodding him
to reveal still more until I was satisfied
he
" 'knew no more. And then I thanked
him and I
" 'killed him.'

"Chintana jerked forward, sharply,
"trying in vain to grab hold again of the
words so casually uttered,
"so easily laid
open,
"laid bare,
"unable to believe he'd
said them in the first place, even if Ezade
"and Iniedia did whimper
"and Micit's
head bent down, her eyes suddenly fixed
"absiderally
"on the worn
"crimstitched
"carpet.
"If only the Social Worker had given
just one indacitation of alarm,
"Chintana
would have put a stop to the whole thing.
"But blinks too of disbelief,
"enforced
probably by her own torpididor,
"could

merely put both women on a temporarey
state of alert.

    "Only his eyes,
                    "grey pools of glum
lake ice, told
              "Chintana what he had
just succeeded in doing
                    "—
                         "he had
involved them and what's more had
now made
            "them
                "—
                    "accountable.

  " 'Soon then,'
            "his always low
"rumbidilling voice continued,
                  "'the
gutters of cities,
          "'curious derelictions
half-buried in abandoned farmlands,
"'poisonous pools lingering in ancient
"'quarries began to speak to me of
                    "'a
way.
      "'And I listened and I
                  "'followed.

“ ‘And after many months and roads strewn

“ ‘in ruin, I came upon a course
to what I would call The Valley

“ ‘of Salt.

" 'There nothing moved and I was
" 'alone.
Anything that had stumbled
" 'upon such
a wideway of grey grief had not
" 'chosen
to stay.

" 'Only shadows remained.

" 'Even

mine left a charcoal smudge

upon those dissected

steeps.

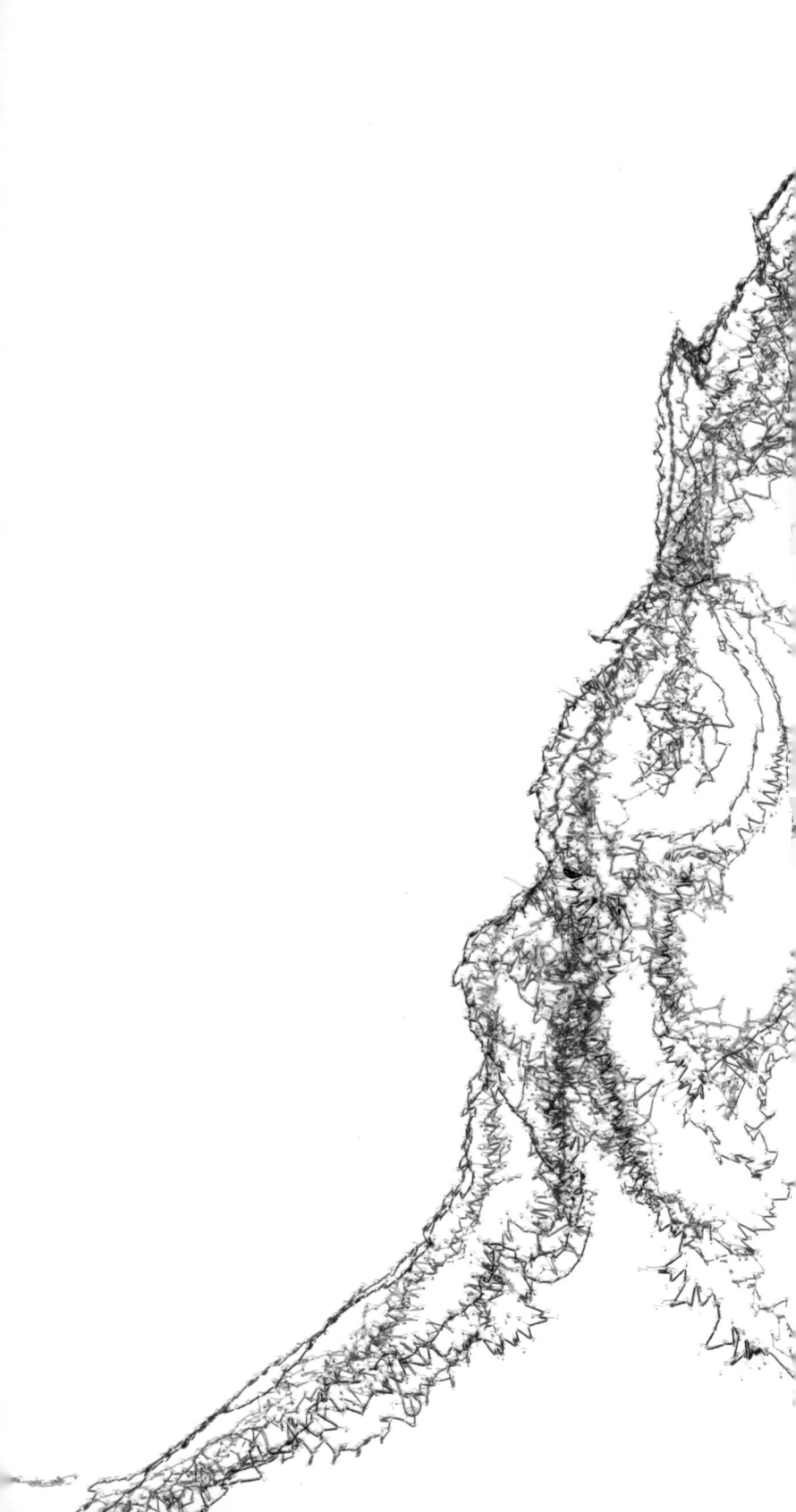

" 'Perhaps

" '_

" 'we

" ' 're

" 'still there today.

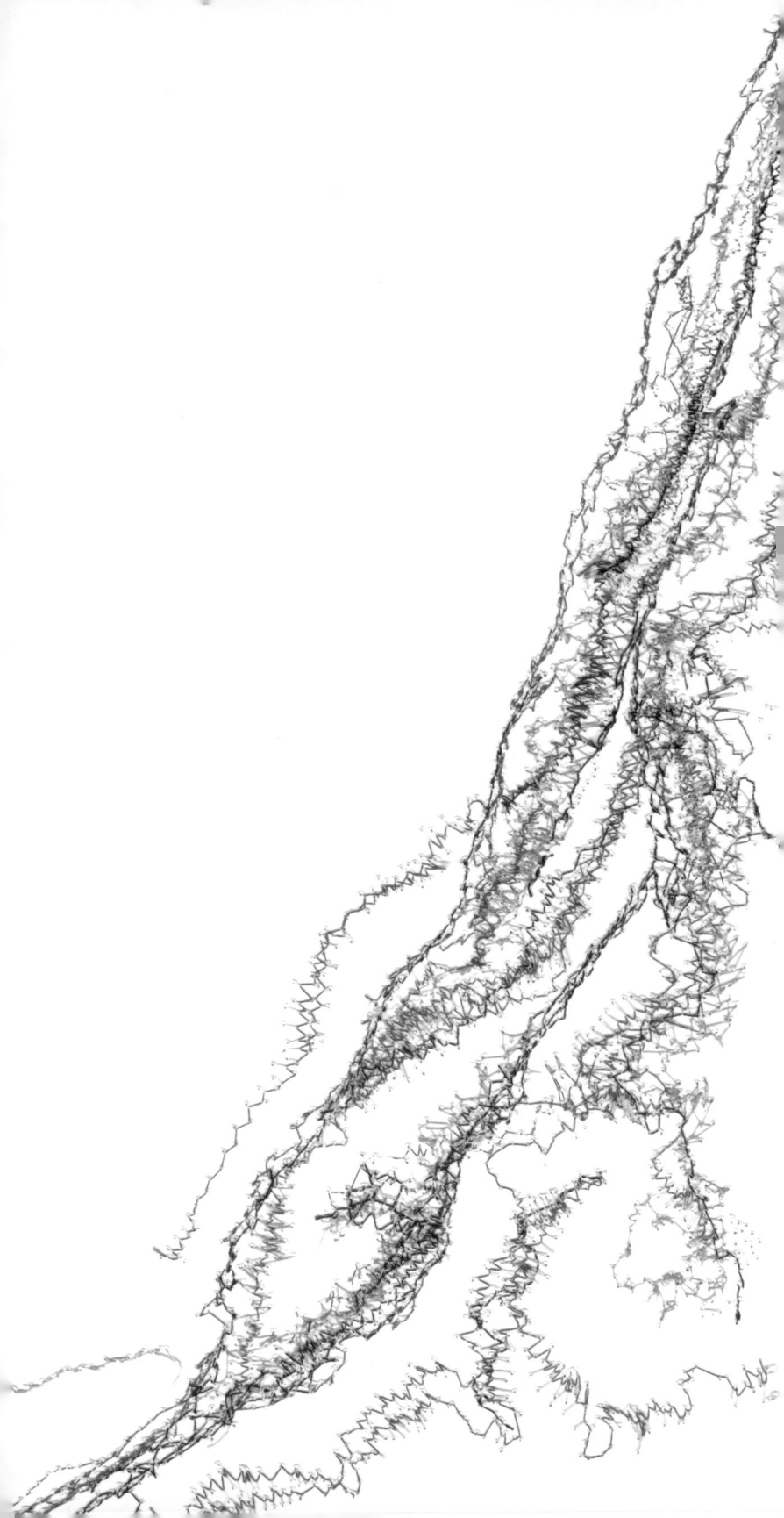

" 'And I saw remnants of many a strange
shadow too. Did you know stars

" 'have
shadows?
" 'They do. And can you
imagine what it feels like to walk
upon the shadow
" 'of a day?

" 'I can't but I don't have to.

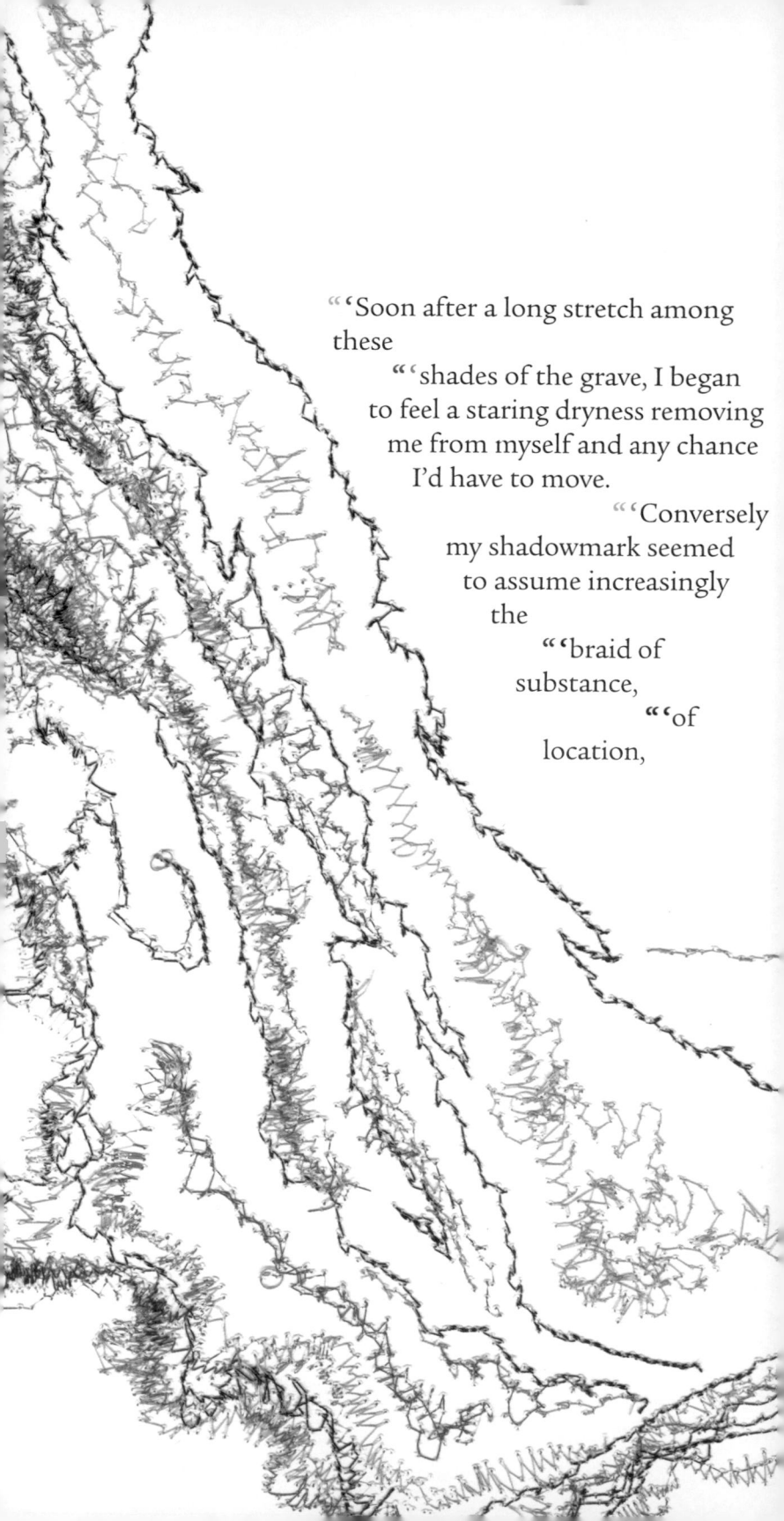

" 'Soon after a long stretch among these
     " 'shades of the grave, I began
to feel a staring dryness removing
me from myself and any chance
I'd have to move.
     " 'Conversely
my shadowmark seemed
to assume increasingly
the
     " 'braid of
substance,
     " 'of
location,

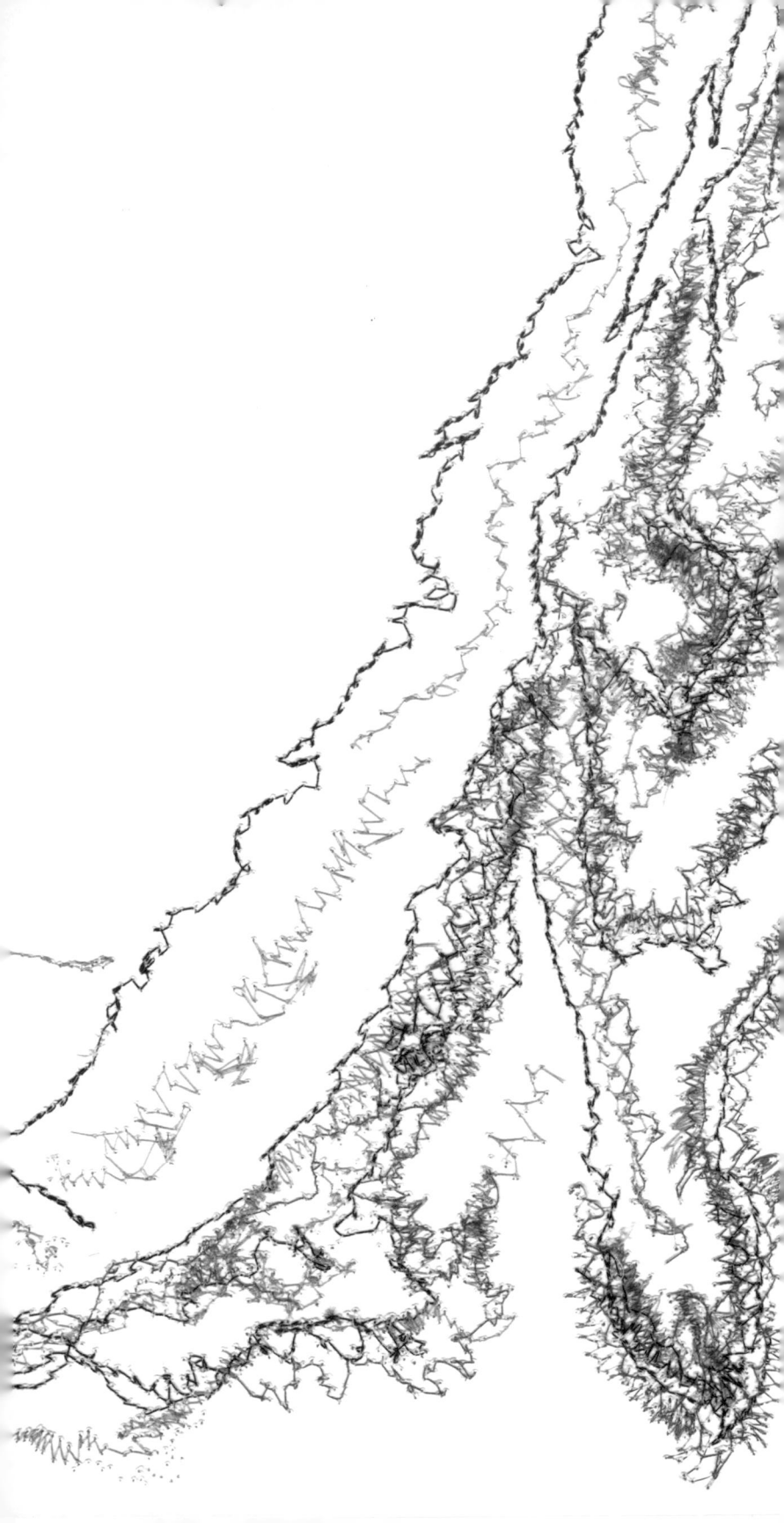

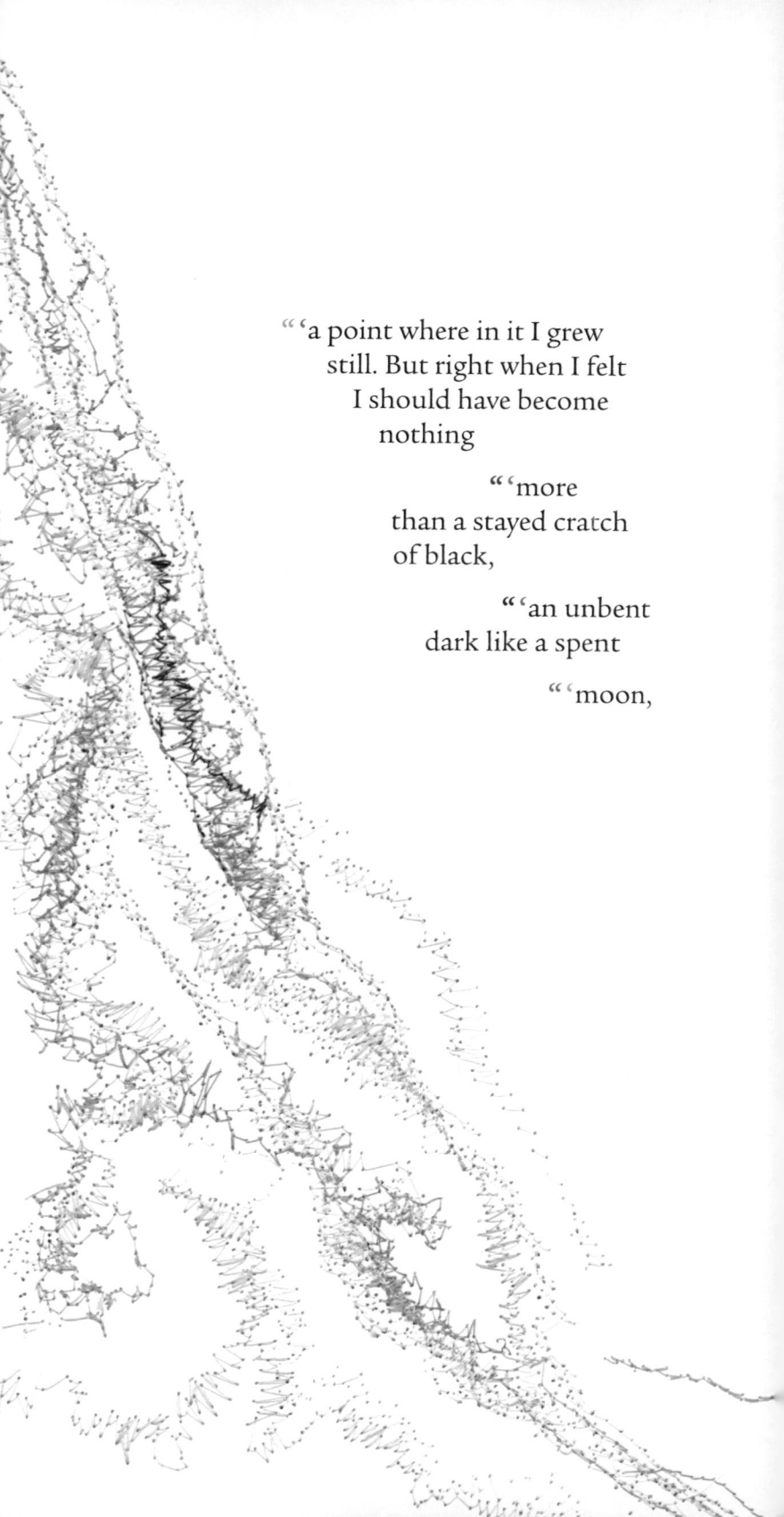

“ ‘a point where in it I grew
still. But right when I felt
I should have become
nothing

“ ‘more
than a stayed cratch
of black,

“ ‘an unbent
dark like a spent

“ ‘moon,

                                      " 'I found I had
left The Valley

                       " 'of Salt and was now
deepening into The Forest of

                                      " 'Falling

                " 'Notes.

" 'So here you say, in a forest,

" 'where
I immediately found plenty of water, I
should also find relief

" 'and rest.

" 'I
thought the same. I even felt happy
enough to sing a few

" 'notes.'

"And sing the Story

"Teller suddenly did.

"Much to the amusement of the
orphans and even Chintana,

"a series
of clucks, trills, sputters and odd clicks
caught in

"whistles in the back of his
throat. He grinned weirdly and before— ❯❯

❝—stopping

❝even hoomed.

"'But this was only the song I sought to sing, not what ultimately spilled
"'out of my lips. That sound was completely different.

"'For you see in the peculiar Forest of

"'Falling

"'Notes, sounds could not hold "'together.

"'Like pearls on a snipped

"'silk thread, they

"'scattered wildly upon

"'the ground.

" 'It did not matter the sort
of sound either. Whether
a melody, a whistle or even

" 'a nick, tick or

" 'clipcrip,

" 'all of it
fell apart. It was even in
the falling apart of
a breeze (though is there

a breeze

" 'if I can still feel it
on my face?)

" 'and in the falling
apart of rustling needles

" 'and seed

" '(though are there even these
" 'if I still can
feel them under my feet?).

" 'Even
the stream I drank from, though
it curled with taste,

" 'I could
only hear in the terrifying way

all the

sound of all

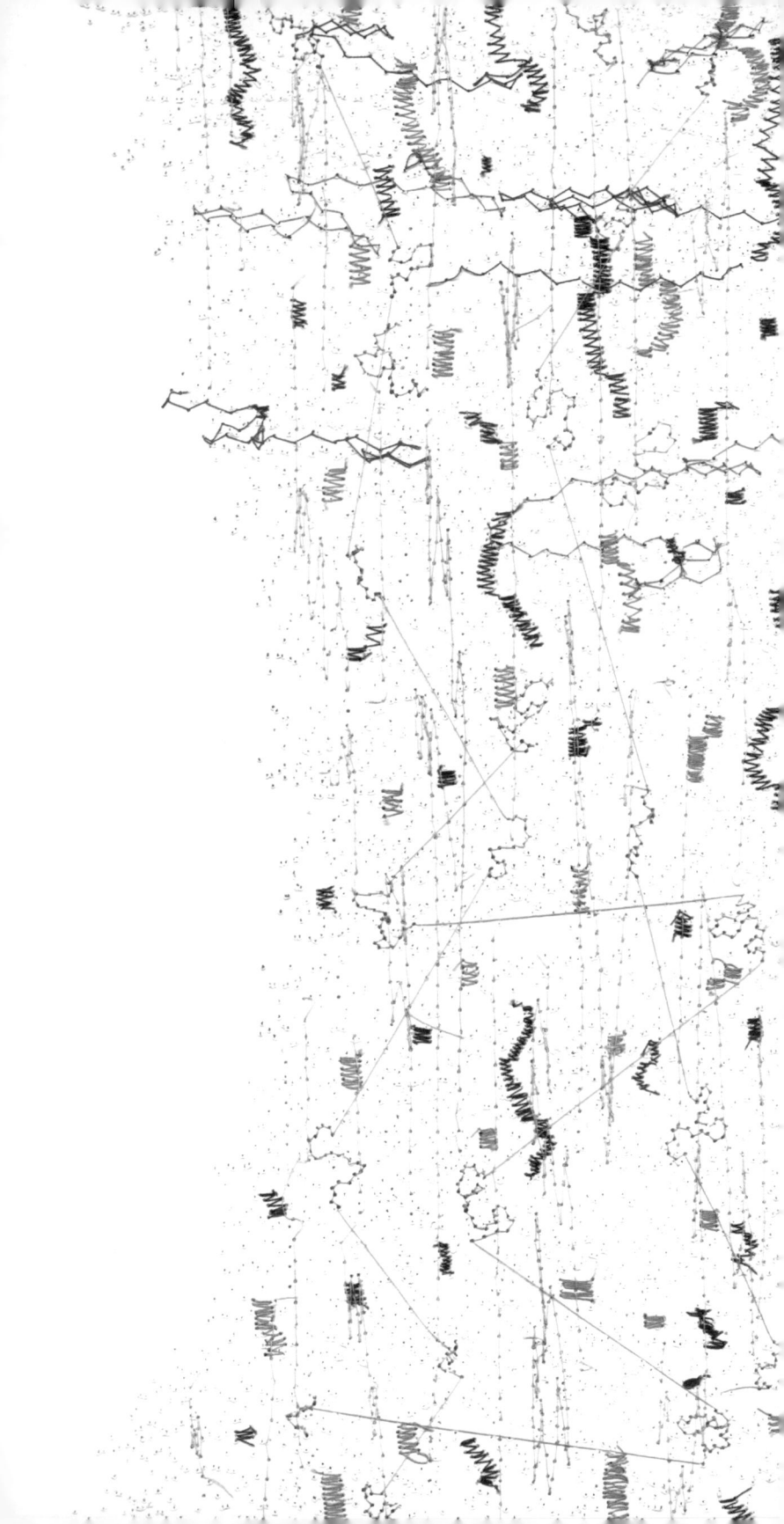

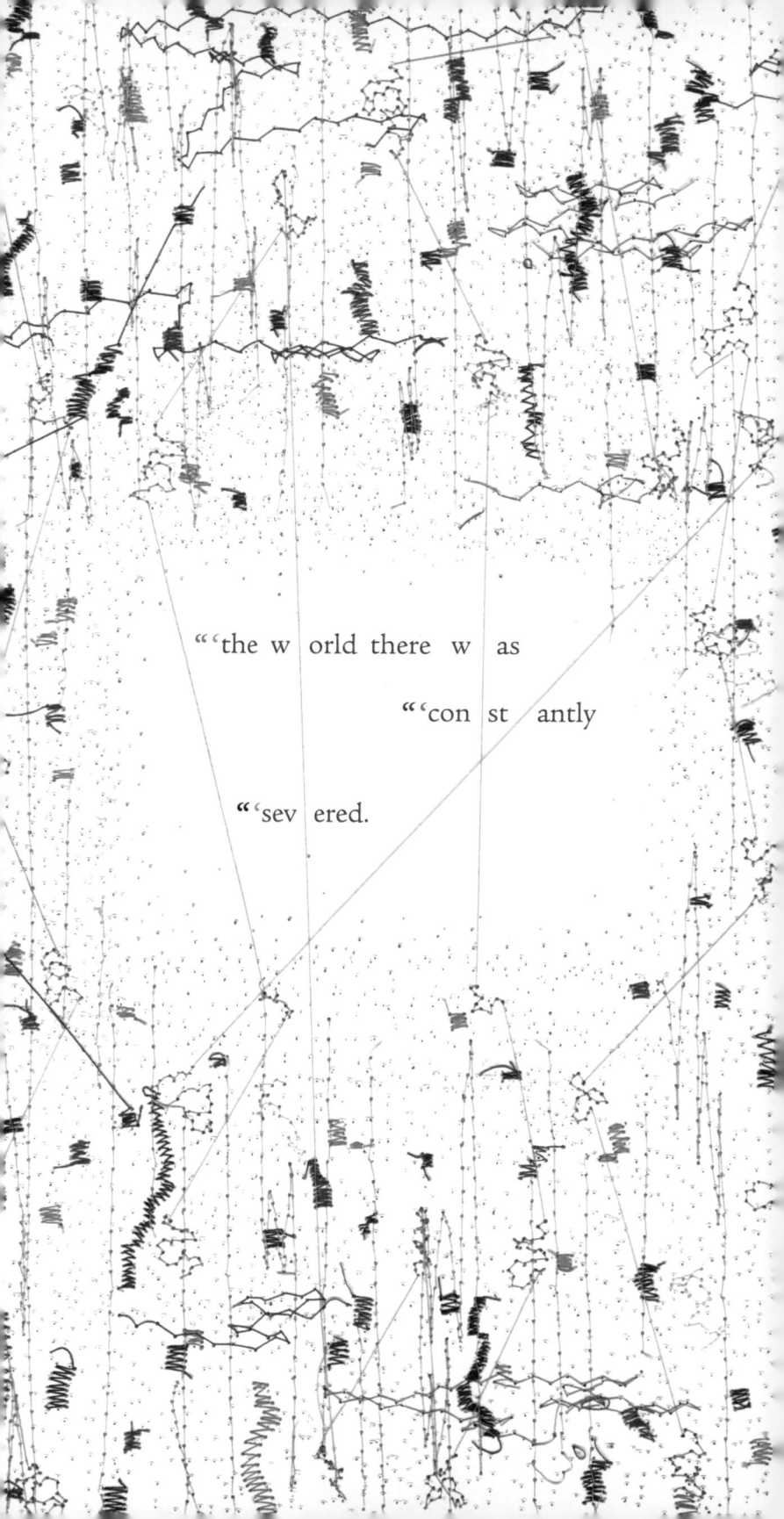

"'the w orld there w as

"'con st antly

"'sev ered.

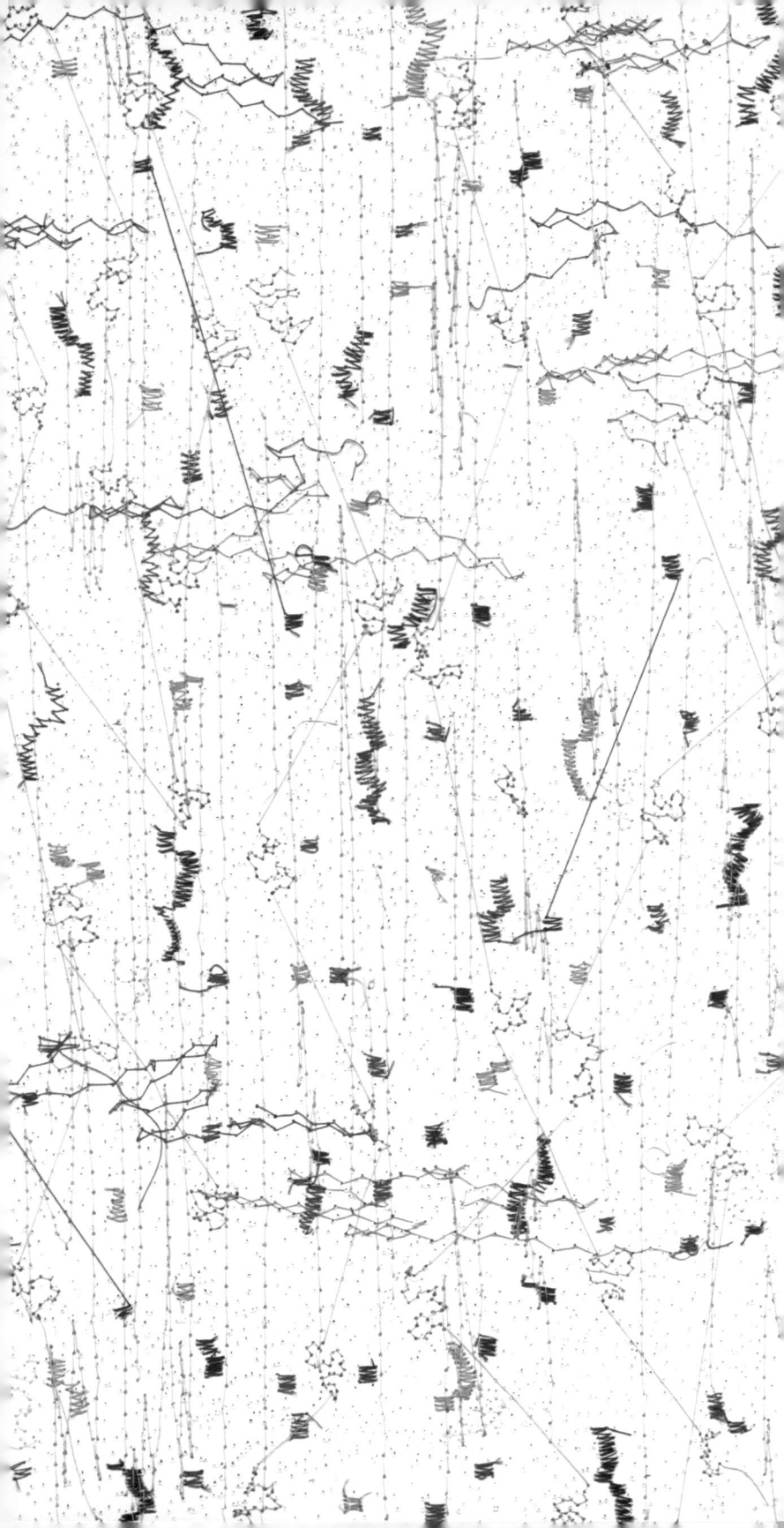

    " 'Worse, what was initially curious and startling became more and

                                      " 'more
terrible, for I began to fear as the sound of my passage and even my own thoughts were

           " 'disremattered, that I was with ever
" 'varied

                " 'velocity going nowhere, that I had come from

                              " 'nowhere, that I was
lost, and soon too like the

                                      " 'matter of my
uncertain

                " 'breath, would scatter among the turns of this

                              " 'unspeakable

                                          " 'wood.'

"Tarff with frowns, Ezade,
                              "Iniedia
"and Sithiss
                "with exchanged glances,
"ittle Micit with a yawn, revealed then
that they too were lost and their
attention
                "scattering.

        "But the Story

                              "Teller missed

"nothing.

    " 'Ah yes, how hard it is to imagine
that Forest
                 " 'of
                    " 'Falling
                           " 'Notes. I know,
   I
    " 'know.' And he lowered his head
"dramatatically,
                    "causing the orphans to
reflexively rock forward.

    " 'Imagine,' he said pointedly, his eyes
still lost in the
                    "downward tumble of his
pose. 'Imagine every sound a
                           " 'sigh of
but one
           " 'thing
                    " 'dying and instead of
 " 'coming one after another it
                              " 'sighs
 " 'a sigh of
               " 'all
                   " 'at once.

    " 'What would that sound like?'

"And he raised his head to look at one
of the windows.
               "And Chintana felt
something within
                    "her part
                         "like a wail.
"Butterflying
          "hope and hold.
                         "Not
neither over the stabbing
                    "pain in her
thumb
     "either,
               "which had clearly
gotten much, much worse,
                         "but over a
horror far more simple

     "—she knew the windows had all been closed.

  "She remembered it clearly by the way
the candles had
               "burned, all five
                         "flames
"arrogantly vertical;
               "impervious.
                         "Now
though, the flames flickered wildly,
dancing on the edge
                    "of annahiliation
as a shriek of wind,
                    "freeze and sky
"whirled around the room.

"Somehow one window was now

"wide

"open.

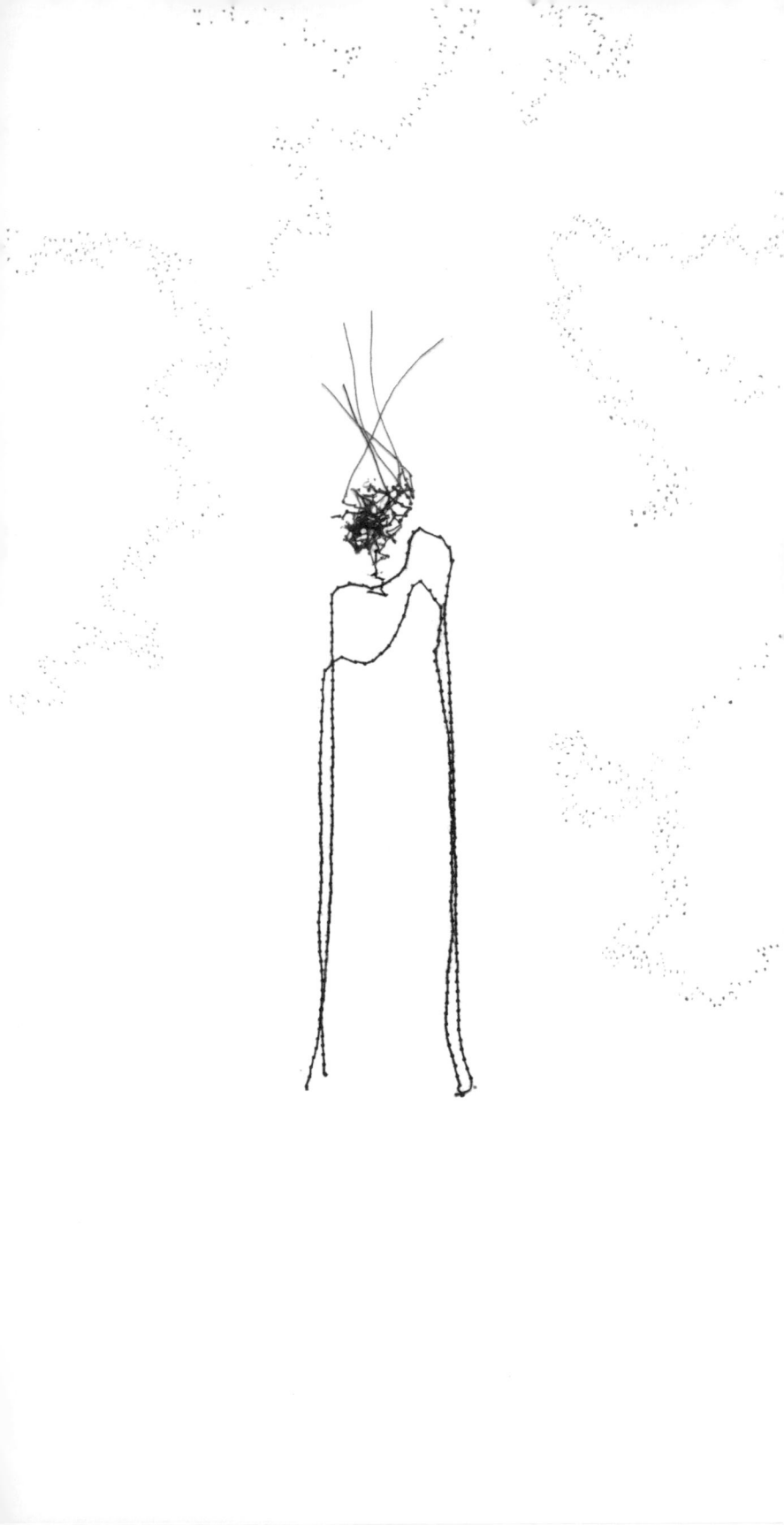

"Already the Social Worker had
                              "leapt
up to close it. Puzzled,
                    "confused, but
"clearly too drowsy to pay too much
mind.
            "The Story
                        "Teller had the answer
but he only
               "looked at the
                              "orphans with
his own questions which they responded
to,
      "and in surprising unaninity,
                              "with a
question of their own—

" 'Then

" 'what happened?'

"'I left gladly The Forest of Falling
"'Notes only to find myself at the base
     of a precarious path rising up
          through twisting leaps of snow
     and looming
                         "'boulders wrapped
     in pale wisps of
                    "'always moving

                              "'cloud.

" 'The Mountain of

" 'Manyone

" 'Paths

had only one path as far as I
could tell. Here at least my
shadow
" 'traveled with me
and the songs I whistled
made sense. In fact the
mountain seemed

" 'just

" 'a

" 'mountain.

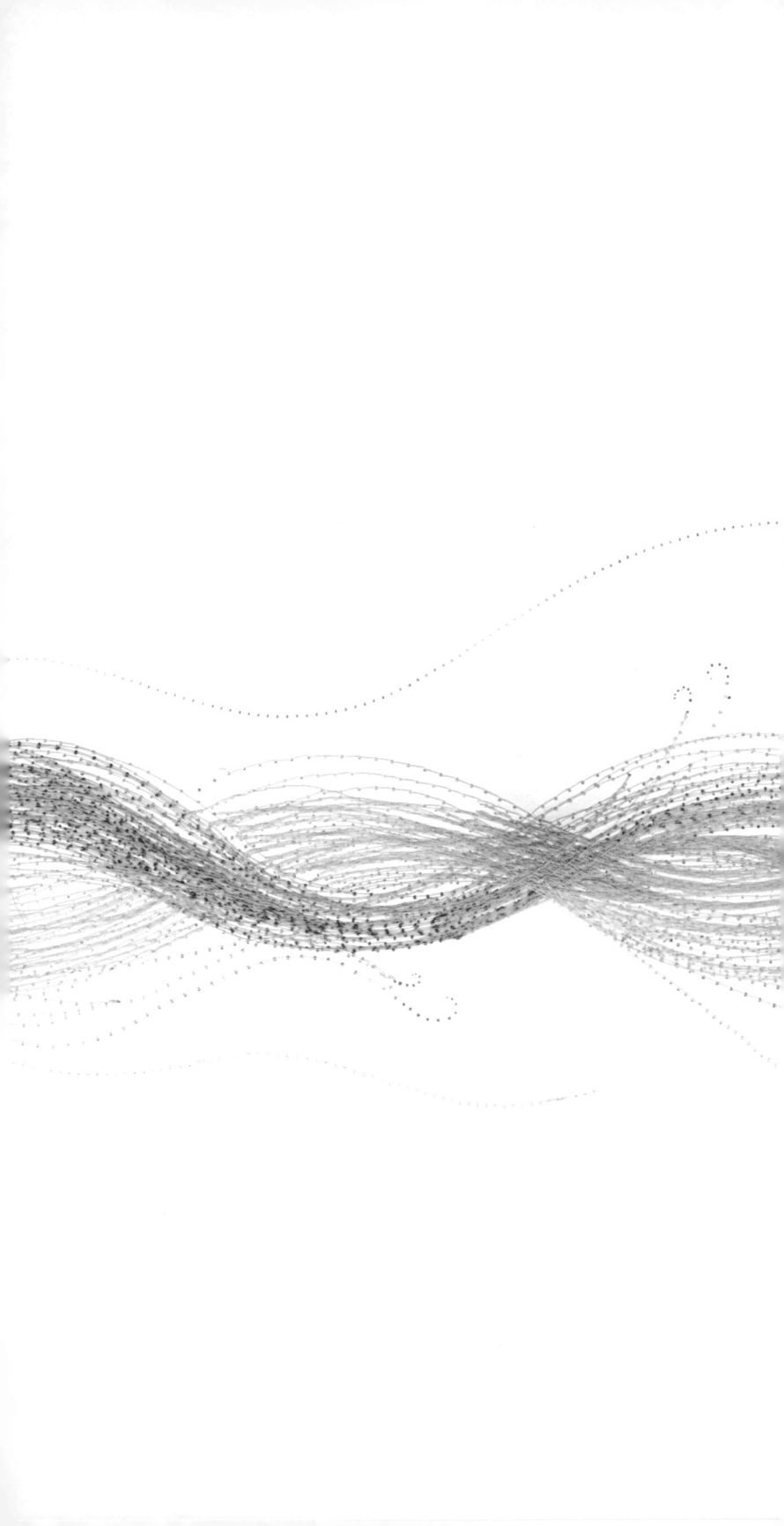

      " 'Only when I began the dangerous
ascent did I start to perceive through the
briefly parting veils of
                        " 'pall and mist another
" 'climber on what I admitted then had
to be a
         " 'second
                " 'path.

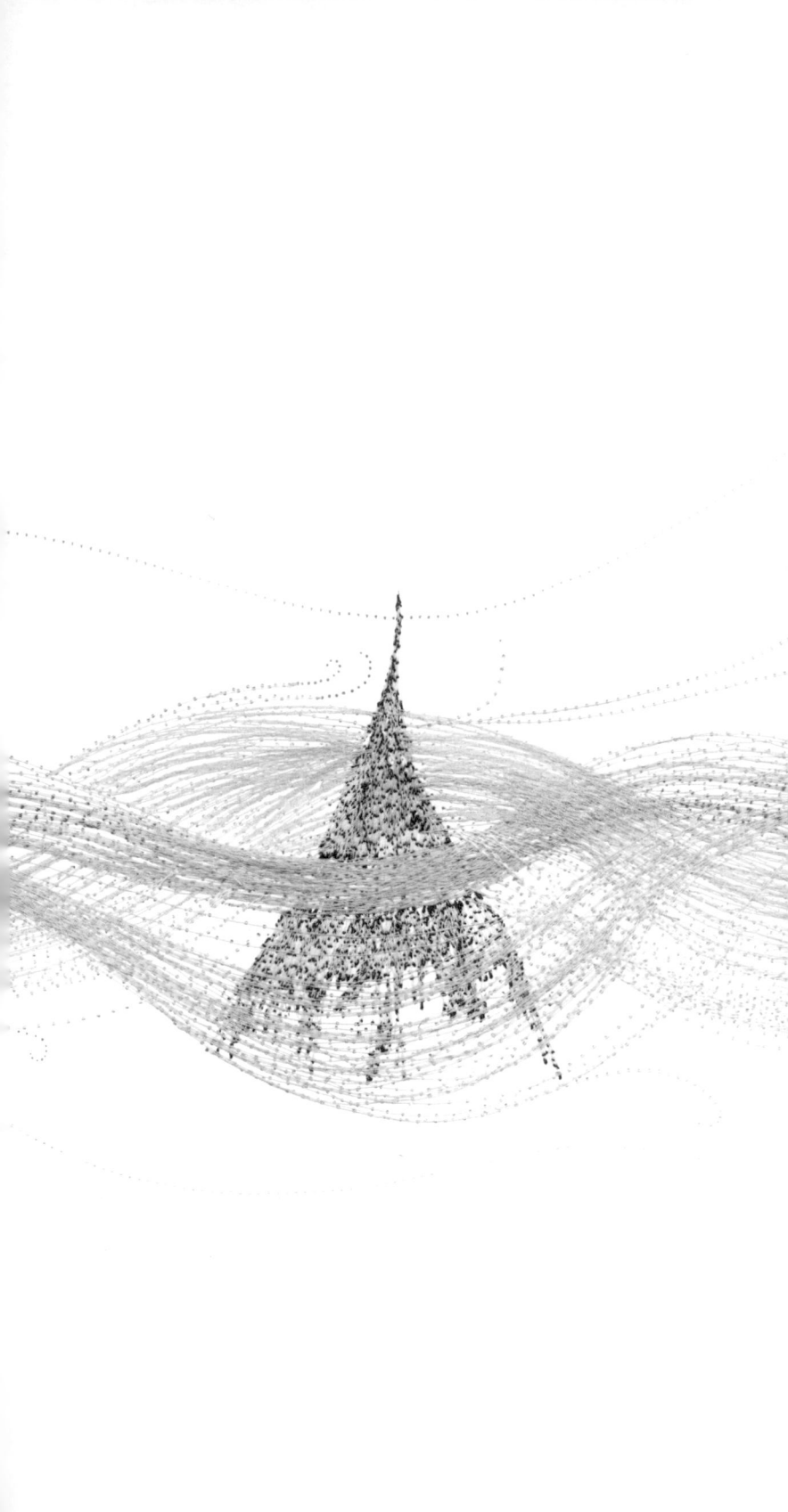

" 'Soon though, the figure was enveloped in white never to be seen again. I had begun to forget the sighting when on a

" 'completely different part of the mountain, below me this time, I momentarily caught

" 'sight of another climber on a

" 'third

" 'path.

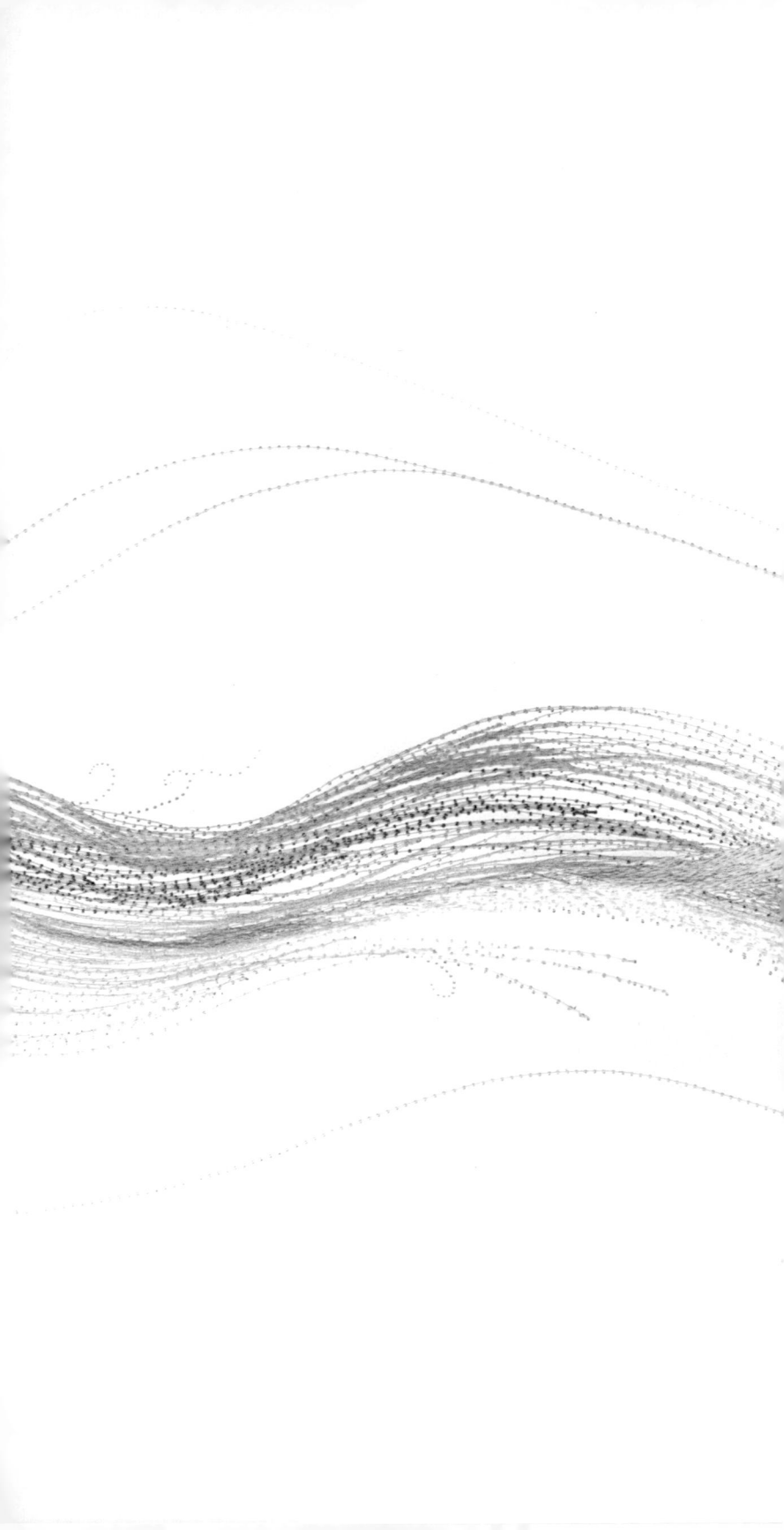

" 'This time I moved down a little in his direction only to watch a twisting sheet of white
                    " 'wipe him from my sight.

" 'Nor was that the last time. On the contrary it was the beginning. Climbers began to
                    " 'pop up all over the
                                        " 'mountain, always on a different

                            " 'path,

                                        " ' 'allways'

" 'swept

            " 'away by mist before reappearing

somewhere else.

" 'Eventually

though, I managed
to get a little closer before the
pale winds
" 'stole

these

solitary

figures

away.

And
it was then that I
could see how all of
them looked
" 'exactly the same,

" 'and not just the same

as one another,

but the same as

" 'me.

" 'And while to this day I cannot really
tell you what took place on The

                                   " 'Mountain
of

        " 'Manyone

                " 'Paths, I

                            " 'understand
still that in spite of so many climbing
figures
              " 'on so many
                    " 'paths, I was
completely
              " 'alone up there.

   " 'Far worse than the
                    " 'petrified
shadows and the falling
                    " 'notes, the
multiplication upon
                  " 'multiplication
of my own solitude
                  " 'brought me
rapididly to the edge of despair, which
is where,
              " 'quite sensisibly really, I finally
found The
              " 'Man With
                    " 'No
                        " 'Arms.

"'First there to greet me though was
"'the soft lull of osage orange and

"'a burnt
hush, surrounding me,

"'softening me.
And how sleepy my strange travels had
made me, so I fell

"'to

"'into a
"'hummock

"'a hammock,

"'hung
"'between two black willows,

"'two black
hills

"'overleaning the edge of a pond
where

"'I slept for three days and three
"'nights.

"'And when at last I woke I saw
on the other

"'side of that

"'pond a
small hut. The door

"'wide open with
smoke drifting up from a

"'chimney
somewhere off in the back.

" 'Upon entering I found only
                              " 'two
chairs at a tiny table supporting one
large bowl of hot
                    " 'tea. I sat and drank
all the tea and when I lowered the
                                    " 'bowl
" 'I discovered sitting opposite me The
" 'Man With No
                    " 'Arms. So startled by
his presence
                    " '—the greyness of his
presence, grey hair, grey whiskers,
                                    " 'grey
eyebrows, greyer still his
                              " 'wide eyes,

        " '—pupooless eyes,—

                        " 'all of him grey
except for his
                    " 'eyelashes, long willowy
lashes rising out and up as
                              " 'if they were
falling away from the earth itself, not
grey at all but
                    " 'a luminous
                                    " 'violet

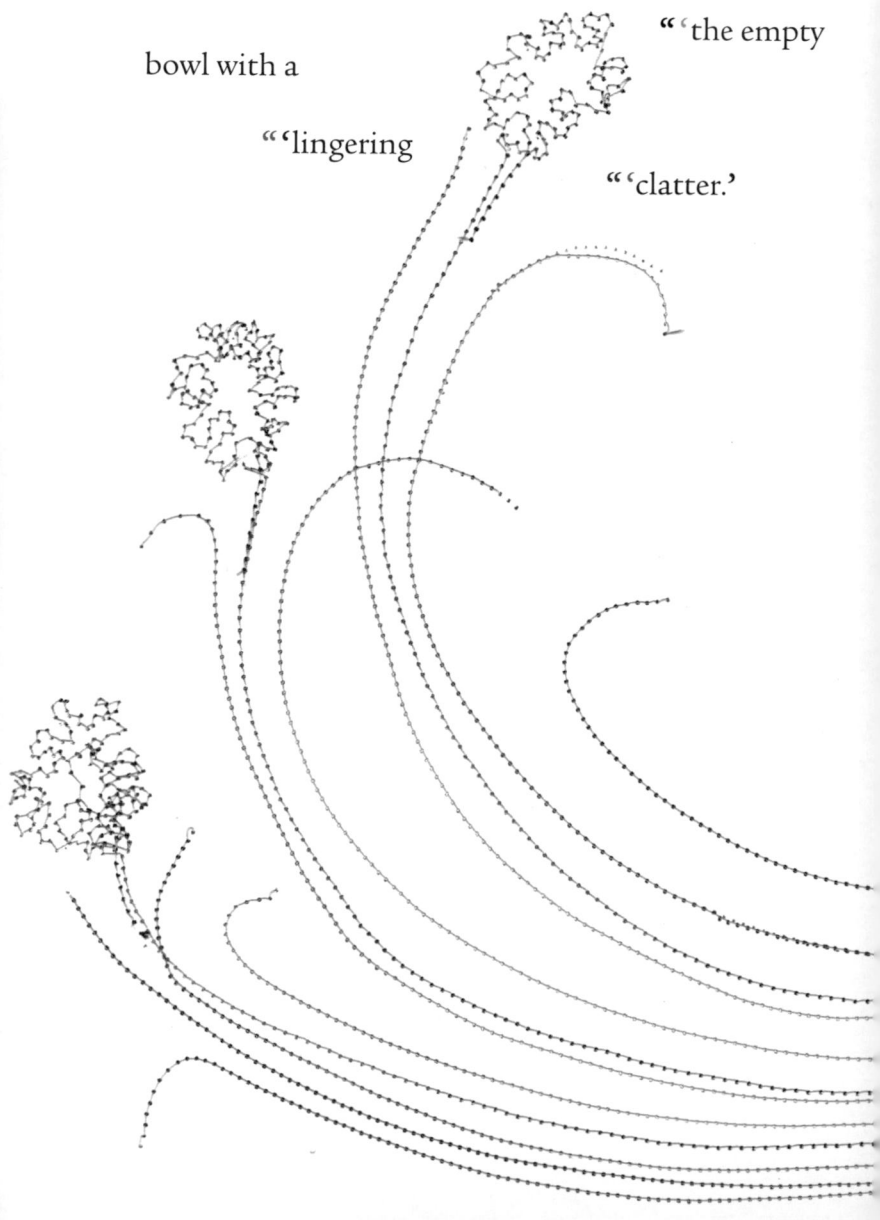

" '—I jerked backwards, dropping

" 'the empty

bowl with a

" 'lingering

" 'clatter.'

"And right then the Story
                              "Teller also
"jerked back, his two hands
                              "pale as
February
            "thrust out from underneath
the silveryblack tunic
                              "to ward off some
wild apparition, his grin twisted into
"mock fear,
            "startling the orphans into a
laughter which
            "in their own way
                              "elicicated
his own chilling
            "laugh.

" ' "*You have come a long*

        " ' "*way*" The

Man With

    " '*No Arms*

        " '*said to me first.*

And I in vain

      " '*trying to locate*

the fallen

    " '*bowl could only nod.*

" ' "*You have come for one of my swords.*"

    " '*And again I nodded / though*
I had not known

       " '*the weapons*
he made were s words.

    " ' "*You know they are expensive but*
your

       " ' "*heart is black and price,*
as much as you know what price
is,

      " ' "*is no matter for you.*"

  " '*I said "yes" this time and The*

        " '*Man With*

  " '*No*

    " '*Arms laughed like a*

        " '*corkscrew.*

66 'There were so many.

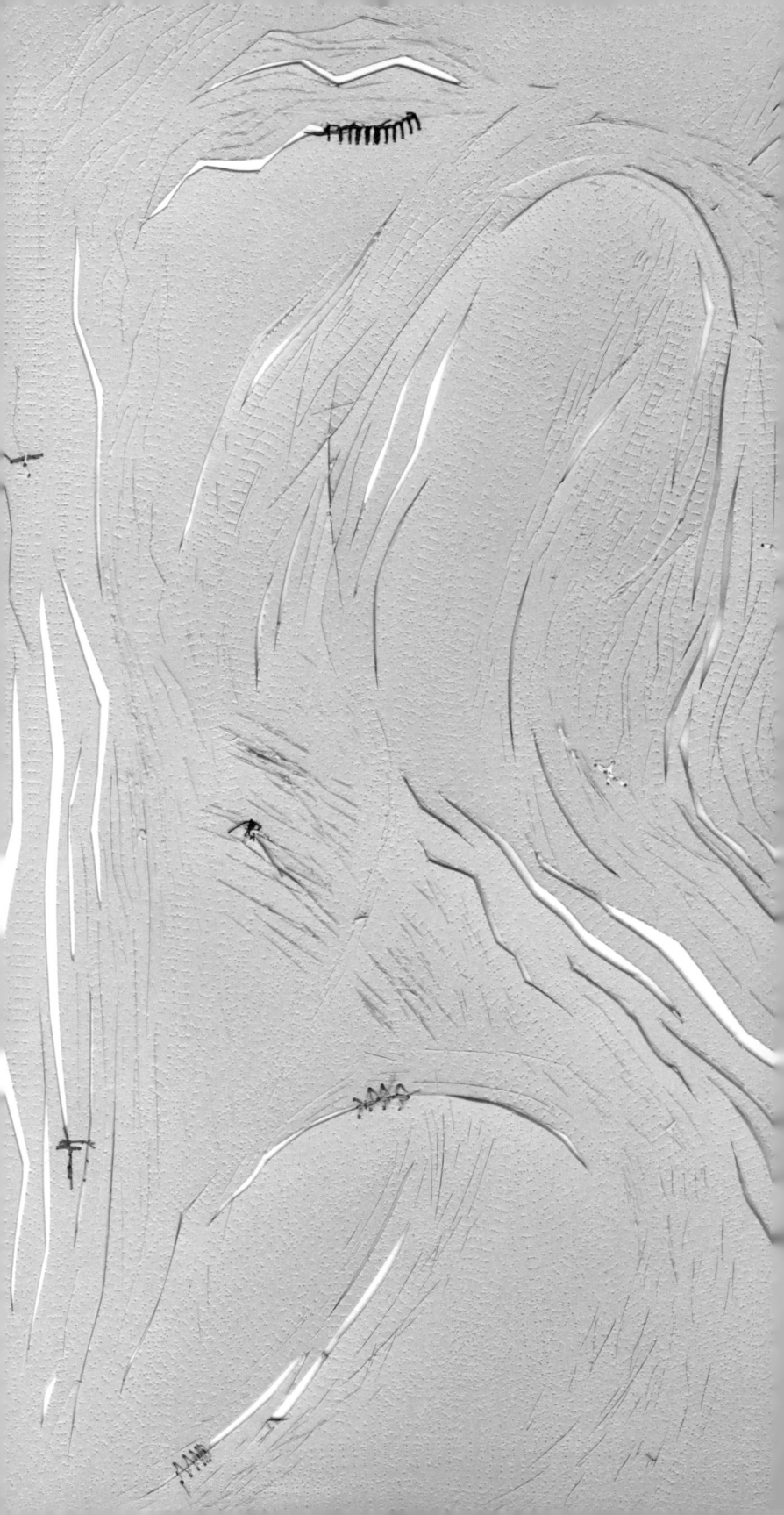

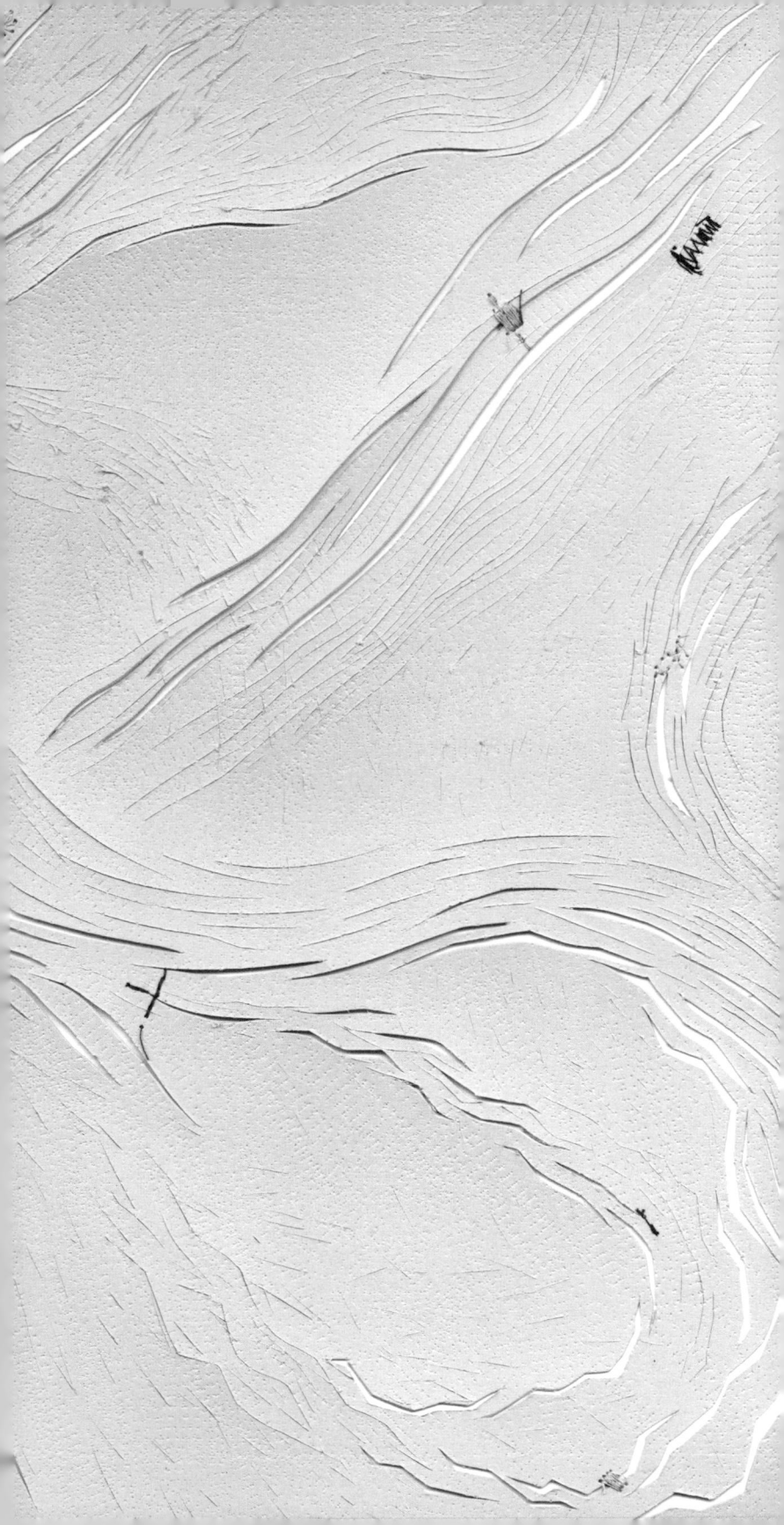

                    Some so small they
could barely reach halfway across one
                                    " 'of
your palms. Some though were wide as
" 'a stare. Some wider
                    " 'than a road.

Some curved like
                   " 'thunder.

"'Some were
            "'straight like the
                          "'sea's
tides. Still others were thin like the
                          "'breath
of a
      "'June dew. And a few I saw waved like
heat
      "'off an August noon.

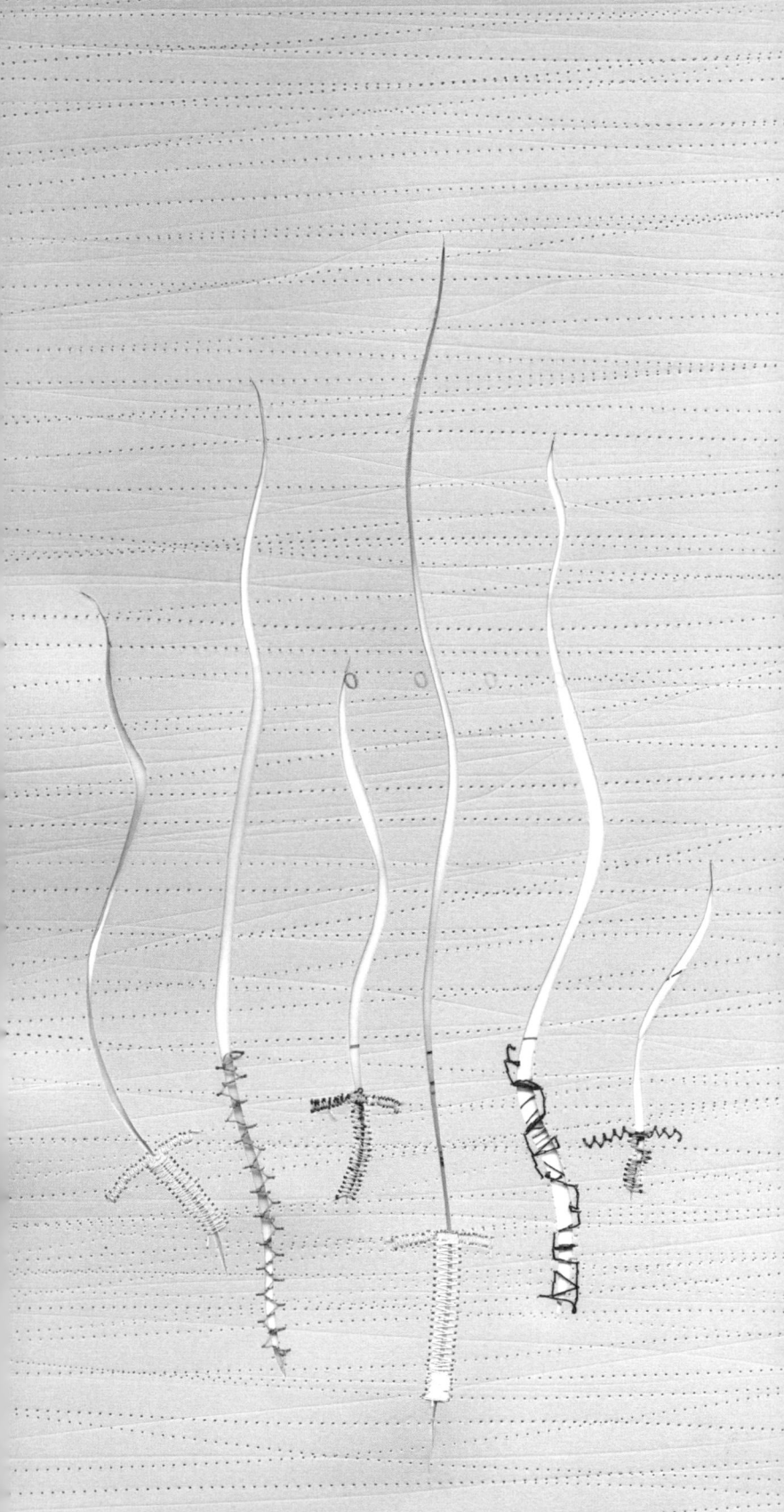

“ ‘But all, as far as I could tell, had the same
“ ‘type of blade—milky white,
“ ‘glossy
and cold, like
“ ‘a fog creeping low across
a morning before
“ ‘a funeral.

" 'In fact so curious was I about their composition, I reached out to
" 'touch
one. And if not for a sharp
" 'click and a wild
" 'fluttering of his violet eyelashes I would have succeeded.

" " *They cut every time,*" warned The Man With
" 'No Arms. "*Every*
" ' "*time.*"

" 'Smartly I withdrew.

" " "*Here,*" he blinked quickly at a blade
" 'at least four feet long, tapering to a blunt
" 'tip.

"This one took
me three winters to make.
" ' "It kills the taste
of salt. The one next to it kills the smell of
" ' "Wild
Lupine,
" ' "Blackberry Lily and lush Evening
" ' "Primrose. There "—

turning to a fat blade suspended in the buz—

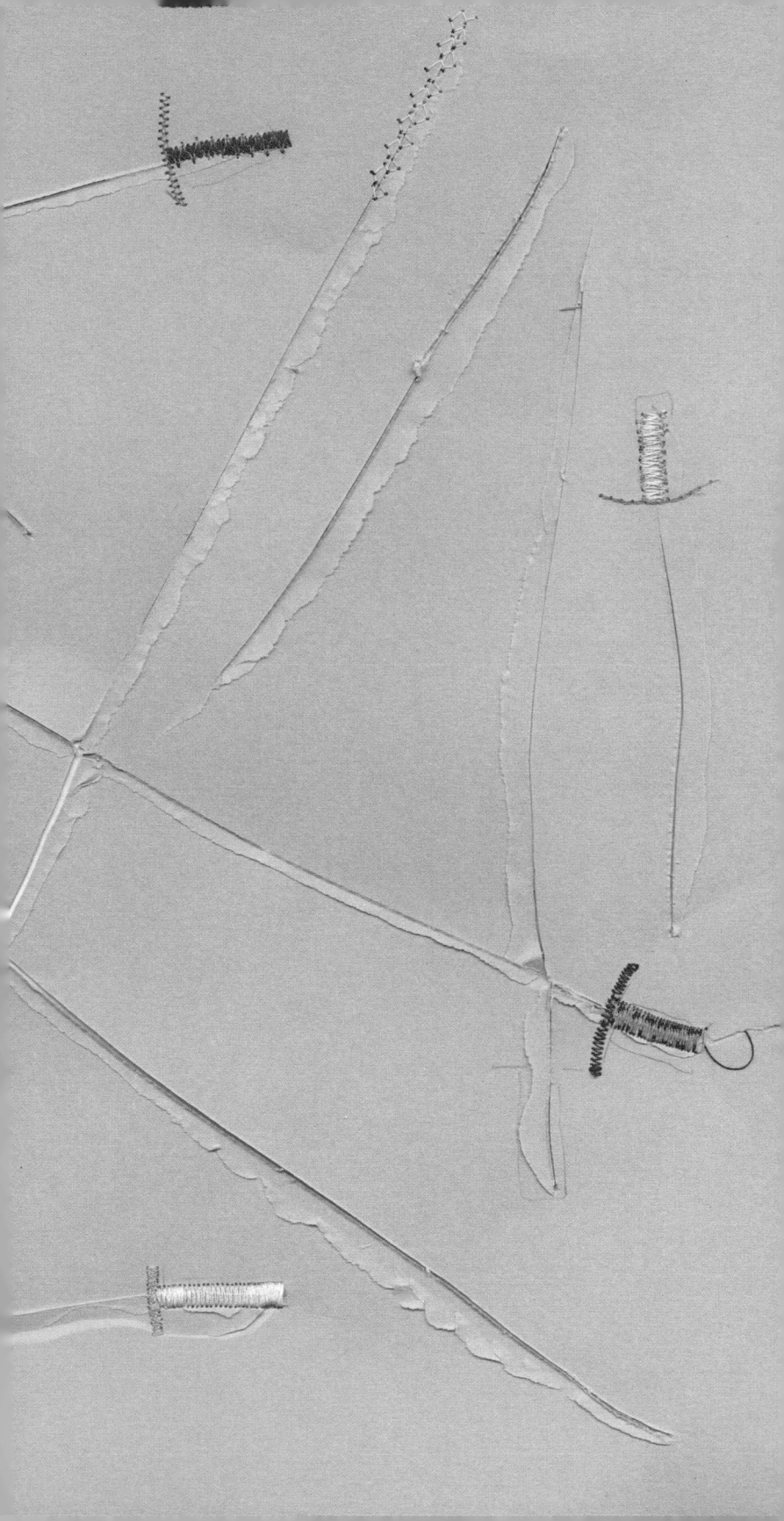

" '—zing grey—"*that one kills the color green.*"

      " 'And The Man With No Arms
  " 'grinned because he already knew the
darkness I guarded and
                      " 'with violent
lashfluttering, turned away from those
tiny cuts and led me
                  " 'on to those deeper
cuts blinking in and out of the strange
" 'shifthickening haze.

" 'Here only a few swords floated.

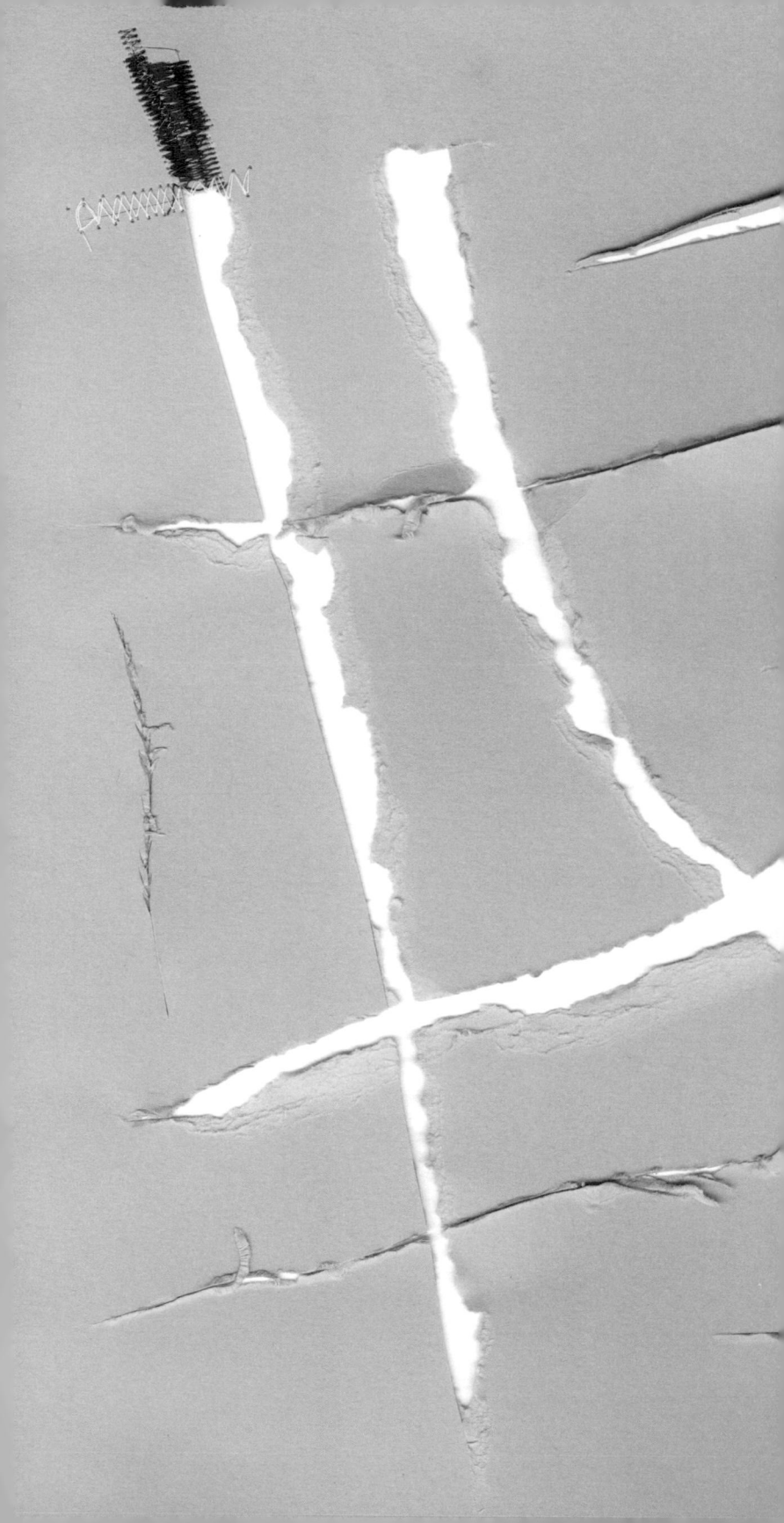

    " ' "*These ones take lives,*" his violet
lashes
        " 'battered.

    " 'But unlike the smaller ones and
the fat ones, they all appeared
                    " 'to be
" 'the same—sleek
          " 'and long—and
" 'bowed like a
        " 'theft.

    " ' "*Ahh, but they're not the same at all.
Closest*
        " ' "*to you is a Ten Year Sword. That
one's*
        " ' "*a Twenty Five Year Sword. A
Hundred above it and there a Two*
 " ' "*Hundred and Eighty*
                  " ' "*Seven Year
Sword.*"

    " ' "And this one?" I asked, tentatively
reaching for the handle until
              " 'unchecked
I actually took hold of it.

    " ' "*That's your Fifty Year Sword,*" he said
" 'oddly.

    " ' "You almost can't see
              " ' "the blade,"

I added, marveling at the way
                              "'the
weapon bit through the air, the way
the finely carved handle,
                         "'bound in a
fine fall braid and beaded
                         "'with winks
of pale pearl, seemed with every swipe
to melt into my
                 "'palm.

   "'"*Oh,*" The Man
                    "' With No Arms
chuckled. "*You can never*
                    "'"*see*
                              "'"*the*
                                   "'"*blade.*"

"' Which I would not understand until I'd
returned and found my
                         "'blade had
dissolved into
              "'breezes and hours.

   "'"But will it kill?" I wanted to know,
"'dimly resenting him now that my
sword
        "'hung once again
                         "'in that
"'filickering
            "'deep.

   "'"*In half a century. From birth to the*
"'"*final second of the fiftieth year.*"

" ' "Every time?"

" ' "*Most of the time.*"

" 'This surprised me—"Why most?"

" ' "*No weapon is perfect. Whatever this blade passes through, it most certainly*
" ' "*will divide, though there is one thing which can stitch and hold the*
" ' "*wound.*"

" ' "What's that?"

" ' **" Ah, your heart is blacker than will ever be told. But that is why you're**

" ' " *here.* **"**

"'Beyond him then, I caught sight of still more swords, though these were
"'inconceivably
                    "'long.

"'"For you maybe," said The Man With No Arms.

"'"For me they are as they are. Some a
"'"mile long. Some
"'"a river long. There is one that is a sky long."

" ' "They kill lives too?"

" ' "*I suppose. One sword will kill*

" ' "*a*
season. One will kill a country. One I'm
making now

" ' "*will even kill an idea.*"

" ' "An idea," I pondered.

" ' "*But those are too expensive for you.*"
And his violet lashes seemed to

" 'tremble
with delight.

" ' "How much?" I pressed.

" ' "*The wielder must die before*

" ' "*wielding*
it."

" ' "But—" I objected.

" ' "*Yes it's tricky. Too tricky for you. As I*
already said—

" ' " '*too expensive.*' "

" 'Then The Man With No
              " 'Arms led
me back among the tiny and wavering
                    " 'swords.

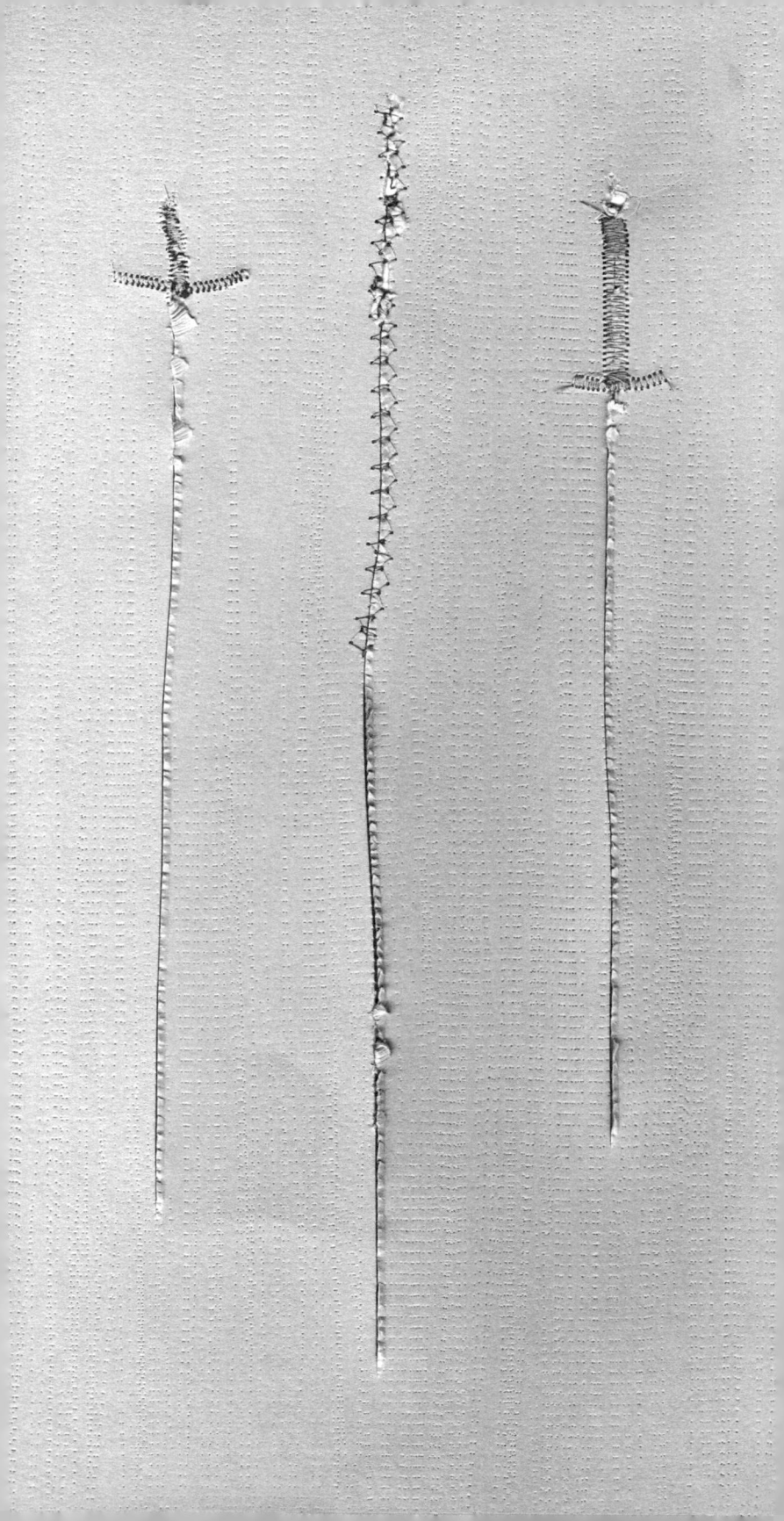

" ' "*These cost a breath you may never take again. Those a feeling you may never shape again.*"

" 'Then his lashes quivered daintily.

" ' "*Beware though as all*
                                   " ' "*are double-edged and come with this warning:*
                                                          " ' "*Should a wound ever fail,*
                     " ' "*you*
                                   " ' "*will vanish*
" ' "*like the blade*
                     " ' "*you wield.*"

" 'But I didn't care.

" ' "What about The Fifty Year Sword?"

" ' "*Your sword?*" His violet lashes twitched
              " 'slyly.

" 'I could not object. I knew too it was my sword. I knew
                           " 'when the handle melted beneath my fingers and the blade shivered
                " 'familiarly along my arm and into my
                " 'past.

" ' "Yes, how much is my sword?"

" ' "*A memory you have which would have*
" ' "*outlived*
　　　　" ' "*you.*"

" 'And before I had even finished
saying "agreed," The Man
　　　　　　　　" 'With No
Arms somehow already
　　　　　　　　" 'held clenched
" 'between his teeth the handle of a sword
with a blade which swayed
　　　　　　　　" 'like a long
blade of evening
　　　　　　" 'grass.

　　　　　　　　" 'Just as
quickly too he slid behind
　　　　　　　　" 'me and I
felt a sting between
　　　　　　　　" 'my shoulder blades
and then a fire and a cold and a sudden
something
　　　　　　" 'seep of hurt. And then my
eyes dried up and they also hurt.

"‘"*There*" blinked The Man With No
Arms, happily showing me what was now
"‘separate, suspended carefully in

"‘the
air:

"‘a single
"‘Harvester
"‘with dark
orange
"‘wings
"‘struck
"‘through
with light and
"‘dapples
"‘of bruised
"‘dark.

"‘"What is it?" I wanted to know.
"‘But
his violet lashes flickered as if now to say
"*no*" and he boxed up my
"‘Fifty Year
Sword and never said
"‘more.

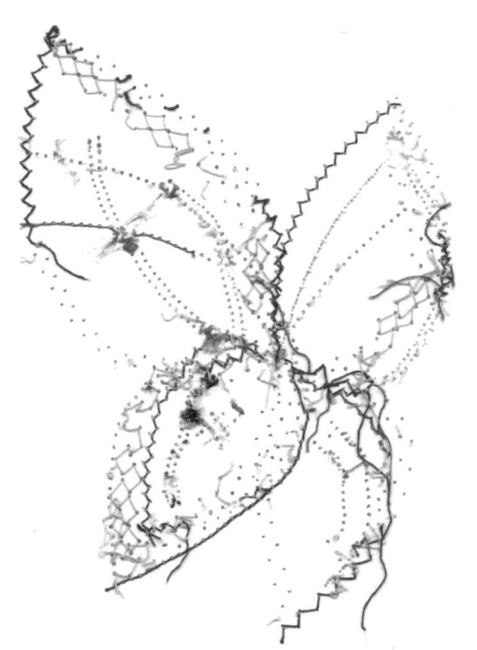

"'And so I descended the mountain of
    "'any
        "'won
            "'paths, crossing back through the
        "'forest of
            "'note before finally making my way
            "'away from the valley
        "'assault.

    "'And only in the years to come would I realize what
            "'he had taken. My heart stayed just as
            "'black and my badness spread
            "'more easily but
                "'the memory
        "'and reason
            "'behind such blackness and badness had
            "'vanished completely.
        "'Which is my
            "'story. There
        "'is
            "'no more.'

"And even if the Story
"Teller had
indeed
"cut himself short,
"which it
seemed to Chintana he had,
"he gave
"no indacitation, only hunching his
shoulders and
"lowering his eyes with a
sigh,
"a sight so soaked with sadness
even the
"orphans
"responded to it.

"Chintana knew better though. She
listened instead to her chest which
guarded
"a more subtle ear, and she
"accepatated the sharpening
"shrill of
her thumb, for even as the Social Worker
snored now in her recliner and the Story
"Teller seemed to recomport himself into
an even smaller stillness,
"Chintana knew
what the
"orphans
"were about to ask

which somehow meant she also knew
                              "he
too knew
              "what they would ask and how
he would answer. In fact the only thing
Chintana did not know
                              "was how she
herself would
              "respond.

  " 'At least get up' she tried to tell
herself, but though
                      "already on the edge
of her seat, as if in
                      "the poison of a dream,
she felt unable to move even
                              "an itsy bit.

    "Tarff grunted then, refusing—
"unable
              "to look away from the long
"box with its angles of
                      "black, and so
asked,

        ""'Is that the sword?'"

    "And of course all five
                             "windows
"were open now and the wind and
falling
              "clouds,
                      "split apart with
falling
              "hail, ripped
                         "into the room
and the five
                 "flames on five
                         "wicks on five
"candles of molasses,
                  "cloves,
                         "nutmeg,
"cinnamon and
                 "ginger shook and
faltered. But no one there could
                         "heed
the candles
              "anymore or understand the
"shadows or hear the
                       "notes or follow
"the paths
              "—not even Chintana who
try as she might could still not wrench
herself
              "free.

"And so Tarff did as he was told,

"lifting the first latch.

"And so Ezade did as he was told,

"lifting the second latch.

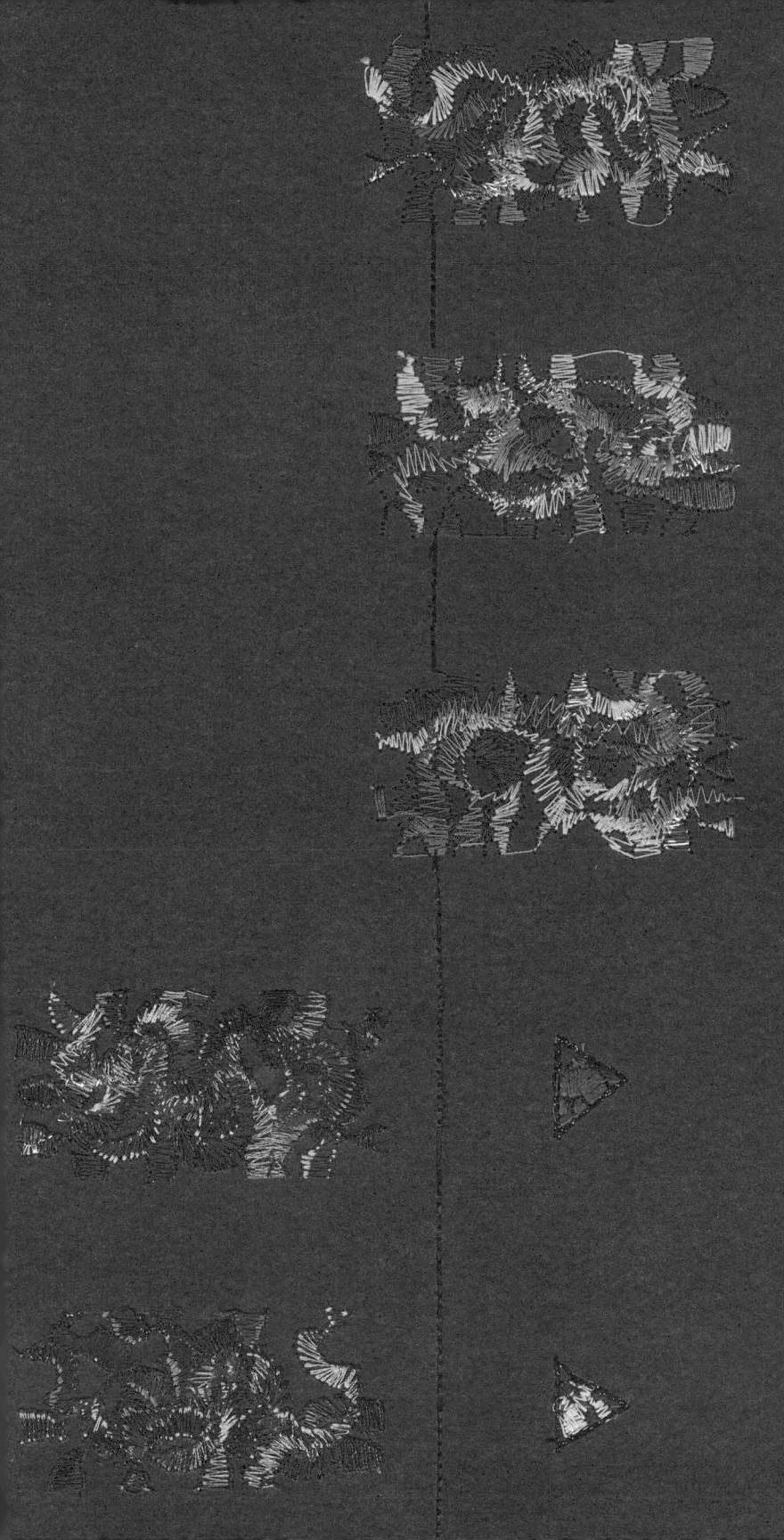

"And so Iniedia did as she was told,

"lifting the third latch.

"And so Sithiss did as he was told,

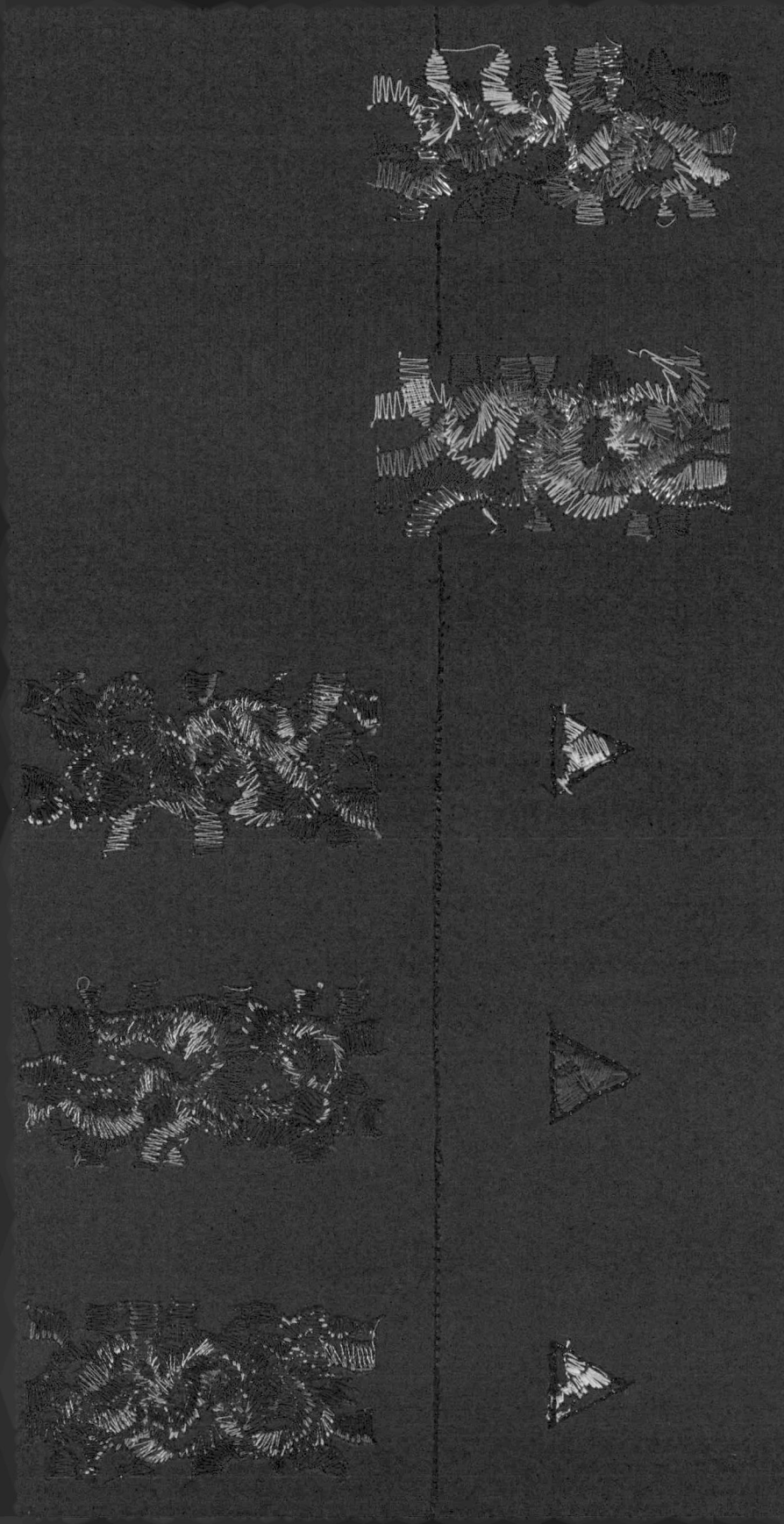

"lifting the fourth latch.

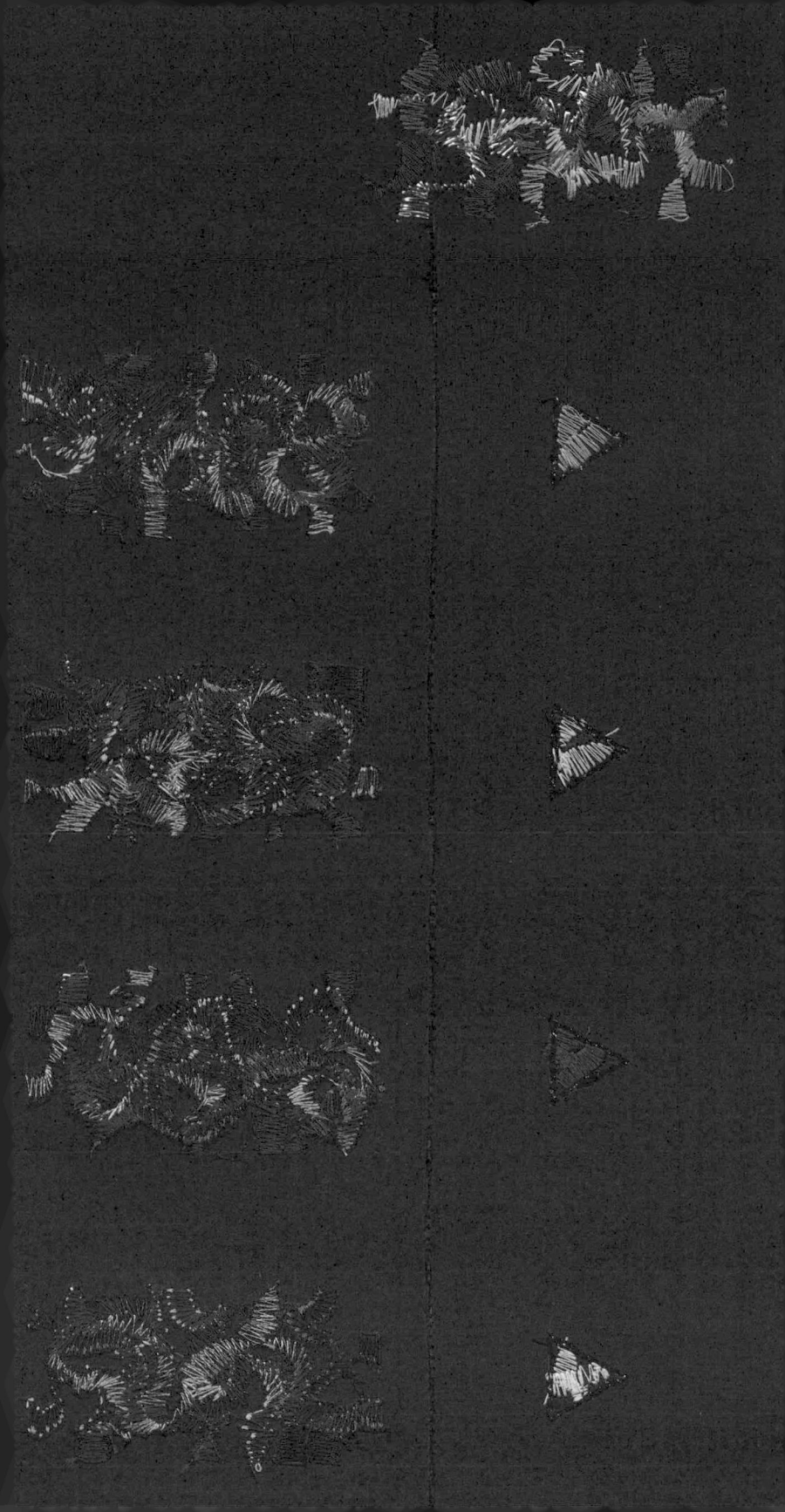

"And so Micit did as she was told,

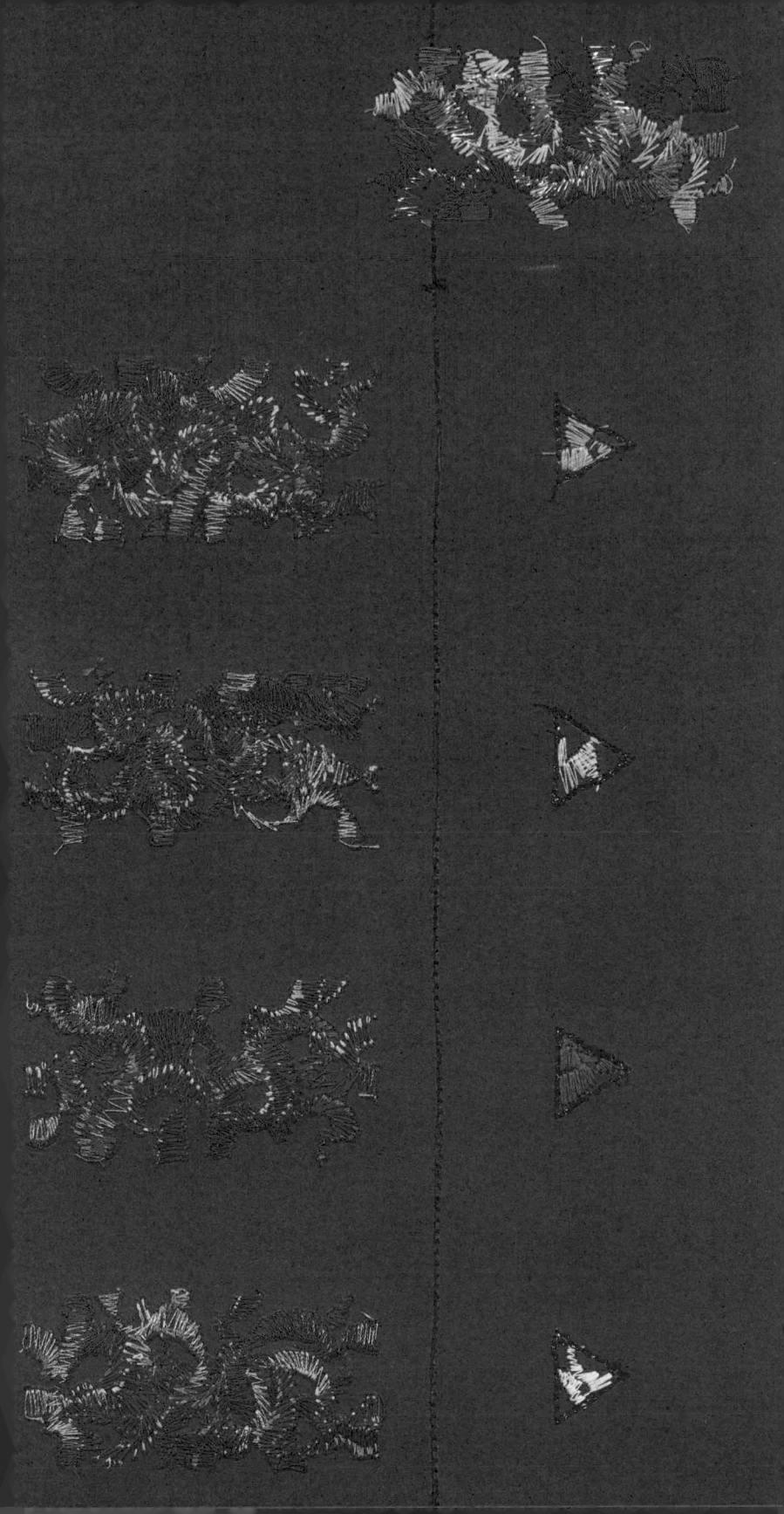

"lifting the last latch.

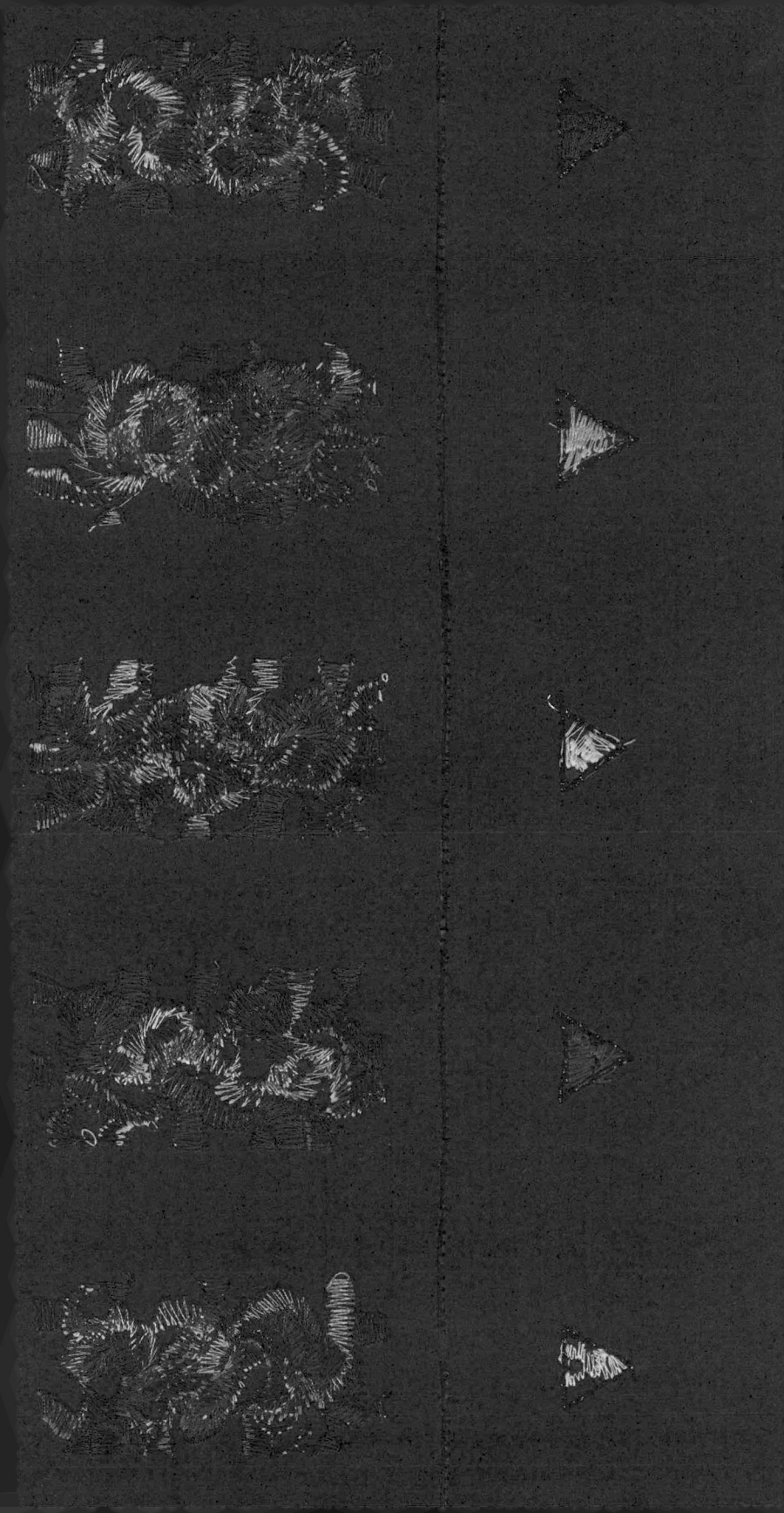

"And then all withdrew as the Story Teller leaned forward and lifted the lid.

"'Hey,' Tarff immediately objected. "'It's empty!'

"'Yeah!' Ezade, Iniedia
                                        "and Sithiss
chorused.

            "Micit even giggled—

"'The bwade is missing!'

"But the Story
                "Teller's lack of
                                "surprise
"reminded them
                "as he quietly reached
in to pull free the finely carved handle
"bound in fall braid and
                                "beaded with
winks of pale pearl.
    "In fact so mesemerized was everyone
by the promise of its
                                "mild bend, no one
seemed to notice how the Story
                                "Teller
was already standing,
                "filling the room,
his shoulders expanding out to the walls,
"the back of his neck pressing up against
the ceiling,
                "all of him
                                "hrowling and
gulking,
                "his shadow falling not from
but towards the terrified
                                "candlelight.

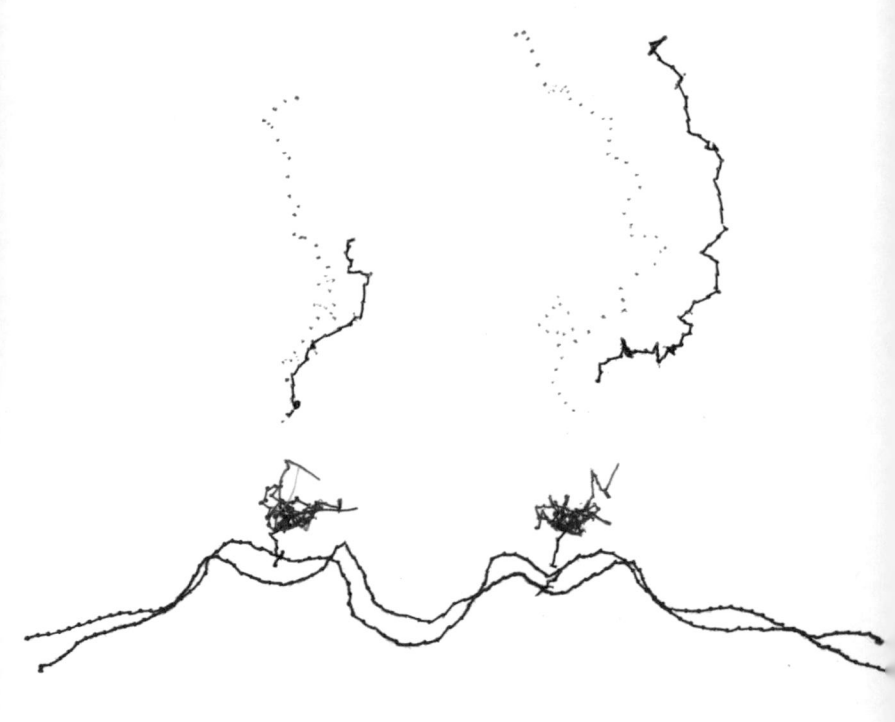

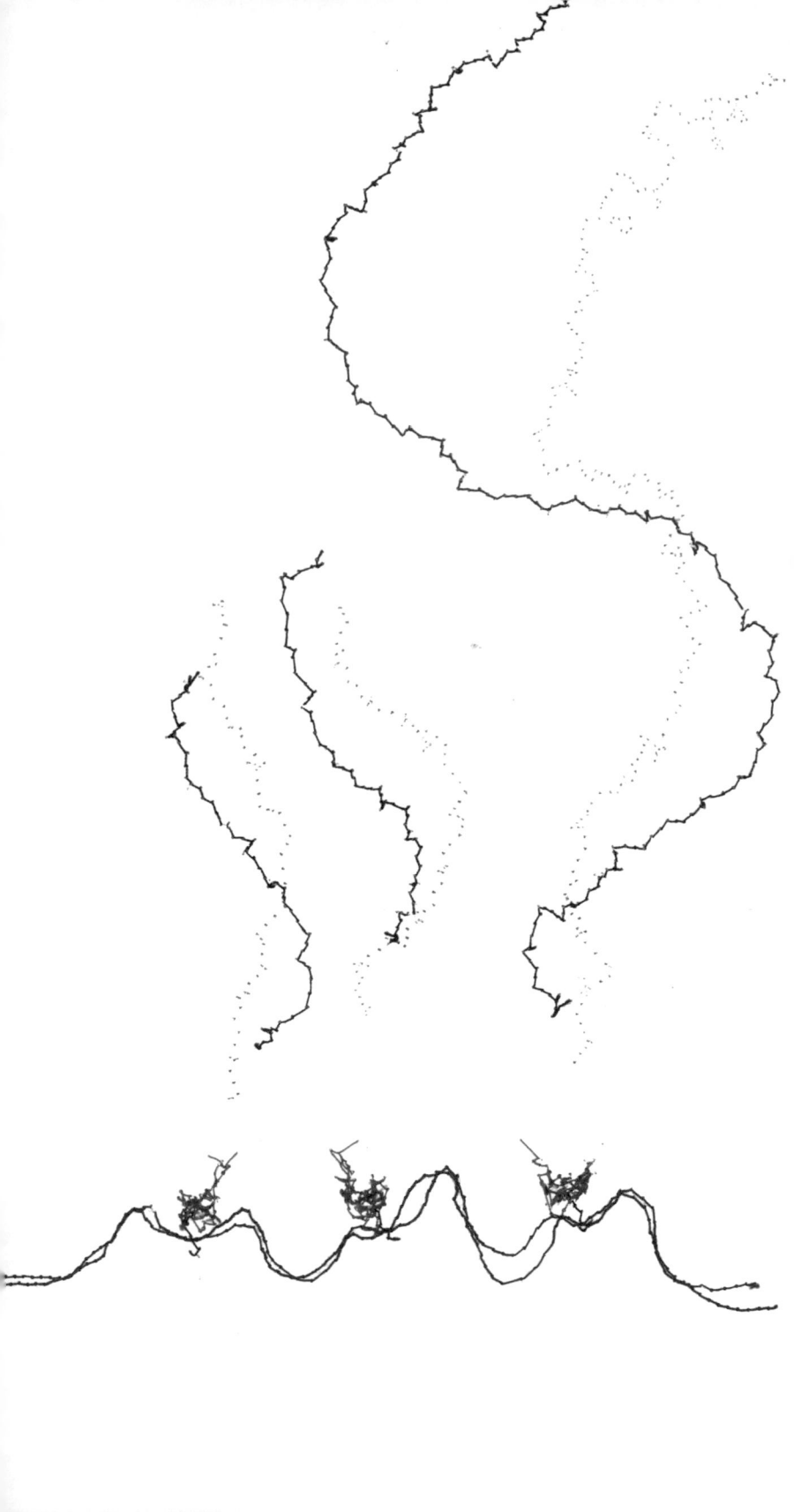

"Where
          "upon
                    "he began to swing
the handle in a wide but deliberately
                              "slow
"arc as if to pass a long blade through
the wicks of those five
                         "candles nearly
six
      "feet away where indeed a yellow
panic there,
                  "perhaps by extraordidinary
coincidence, momentarily cowered
                                  "into
small rounds of blue and drowning
smoke.
     "How his lips gleamed sharp
                              "red then
as, gripping
               "the handle with
                         "both
hands, he raised it high above his head,
"twisting his shoulders away,
                              "though
never relinquishiding his gaze
                              "—fixed
      "—awfully

          "on the orphans

                    "still seated at his feet.

"Insitinctively Tarff and Ezade jerked their arms up in front of their faces.

"Iniedia yelped. Sithiss leaked out a

"whine.

"But Micit wailed.

"Chintana forced herself then from her chair but she was

"too—

"far too

"late, the Story

"Teller already swinging down and across the necks of the five orphans, "a vicious and terrible round

"with even worse implatications if his hands hadn't clutched

"nothing at all;

"for indeed

        "at the height of their ruin
"yet before their crime,

                "they,
                    "those
hands,

     "pale as February had been so,
"so seamlessly so,

            "and so expertly so,
"stripped clean,

        "replaced with a ladle of
angry air.

" 'Tripe. Hogwash. Baloney and hooey,' Belinda Kite spat loudly, striding forward,
"the handle now
"somehow miricallously
"in her possession.
"How easily too it seemed she had just reached
"out of the shadows and plucked free from his glacial grasp
"the end of his story.

"Despite herself, Chintana was "overjoyed, even if she also wondered what on earth could have prompted "such a display of uncommon heroics. Had some protective instinct
"suddenly insisitated she act on behalf of the orphans or was it just more evidence of
"Belinda Kite's natural predespotician to spoil "a pretty gripping moment?

"Whatever the case, Belinda now dangled
"the curious
"handle between her two very nimble fingers—

"'It's time to cut out such doodoo.

" 'Look closely my children, this is nothing but a bit of

" 'phoney ph o ot e y.' Where

" upon

"Be linda K ite,

" to fu rther subst an itiate h er claim,

"proceeded to swing, and

" to no effect,

"stab, gash, cross,

"flay, chop, slash,

"cube,

pare, lop,

"perforate, puncture, slit,

"pierce, sunder, and jab t he

"handle

"at her self,

all over

"her self, around herself, a cross,

"through,   making

          "sure   to
                                crosscriss her

knees,

                              thighs

     "and   waist, dice

     "her   fin   gers, wrists,

"elbows   and   arms,

          "sectioning,

"filleting   and

     "lancing   neck,

jaw,

          "nose,

               "ears and

                         "scalp.

A   com   plet   e

          "hacking   and dissecating

     of her

               "body

part of   her un cut,   "entire, no
                              "un   tou ch ed
or

          "un   mincti   cated.

"And everyone there, though
                              "no one
else would have admitted the possibility
that someone else had
                    "seen so, or
                              "saw so,
       "caught a glimpse
                    "now and then of
something
              "slippery,
                    "biting through
the air,
       "white and vague,
                    "like a slow
cold fog creeping across
                    "an evening
after
       "a burial.

"Belinda Kite sent the
                              "storyteller
"packing with his long box of black
"angles. And leave
                    "he did in the
aftermath of the blizzard
                              "even if no one
saw him
              "go.

    "The Social Worker had loaded the
children
              "into the van only to discover it
wouldn't start.
                        "Chintana's jumper
cables didn't help.
                        "A County Clerk
called a tow truck.

    "Someone then remarked that the
night felt wide and
                        "deserted.
                                    "Without
creature
              "or comparison.
                              "Rot of wood
and mud mute.
                    "The kennels empty.
                                          "Not
even a wing flinging its shady
                                    "whisper
over fields
              "void of paw print, step or
even moon.

"In the kitchen a Caterer informed a just-arriving

"and very-harried School Teacher that the children had left

"long ago. To which this very late

"teller of stories,

"the only one Mose Dettlesome had hired,

"sighed heavily, abandoning at last his plans for animals and

"stormy nights in favor of a bowl of spaghetti,

"—farfalla!

"a wedge of pear tart

"and eventually a deep glass of Scotch all while he cursed his

"sedan and the early freeze,

"though still managing to make the Caterer giggle with limericks about "cutting the cheese.

"But the Caterer was wrong. The children hadn't

"left

"just yet and as mindight approached they were

"upstairs again in the storytelling room, waiting for their ride,

"revoluting against sleep,

peering down at the guests gustering about
outside
     "in the snow on the
          "back
patio
    "where, with most of the caterers
"cut loose hours ago,
       "a skeleton crew
did their best to fast uncork
         "bottles of
sugary champagne and
       "fill brimhigh all
those platic goblets.

  "Somewhere someone began to
          "sing.

   " 'None of that, thank you,' Belinda
Kite snapped. 'Just raise up the bubbly
and choke
     " 'it back.
        " 'Happy Birthday
to me, spoken, will do.'

  "The woman with topaz clamped on
her ears was the first to scoop a second
"fill.
    "No doubt to take the edge off.

  "Many were very drunk but no one
was
    "cut off.

"Chintana without a glass
                    "of anything
  "to fortipify herself against the biting
cold didn't know
                 "what to make of why
everyone else,
                "including herself, had
agreed to stand
                 "outside. Belinda Kite,
because she claimed to adore the snow,
had demanded her
                 "toast take place in it.
And for some reason
                 "everyone obliged
though Chintana could see not many
liked it and even less liked
                 "Belinda,
focusing instead on the
                 "champagne,
"the clicking of plastic on
                 "platic rim,
  "anything and everything but
                 "Belinda.

“And then swiftly by swiftly,
            “as
the moments edged closer to midnight,
“closer ever to Belinda Kite's fiftieth
birthday,
            “Chintana with whirls of
“butterflies suddenly panicking inside
her,
        “so oh so
                “sunflower wild, began
                            “to
understand something she could not
have prepared herself for.

    “No matter Belinda Kite had
desacreated everything that had
mattered to Chintana,
                    “everything
that had made sense.

    “No matter Chintana now moved
through light and stream a grave.
                        “By
tents of indecent rage.
                    “Chintana still
chose not
            “to abandon Belinda Kite.

"And so as seconds

        "flickered

seconds

    "on seconds

       "from twelves,

"like long violet lashes,

       "Chintana

     forced herself from   the promise

      "of

        "infliction's

           "peace.

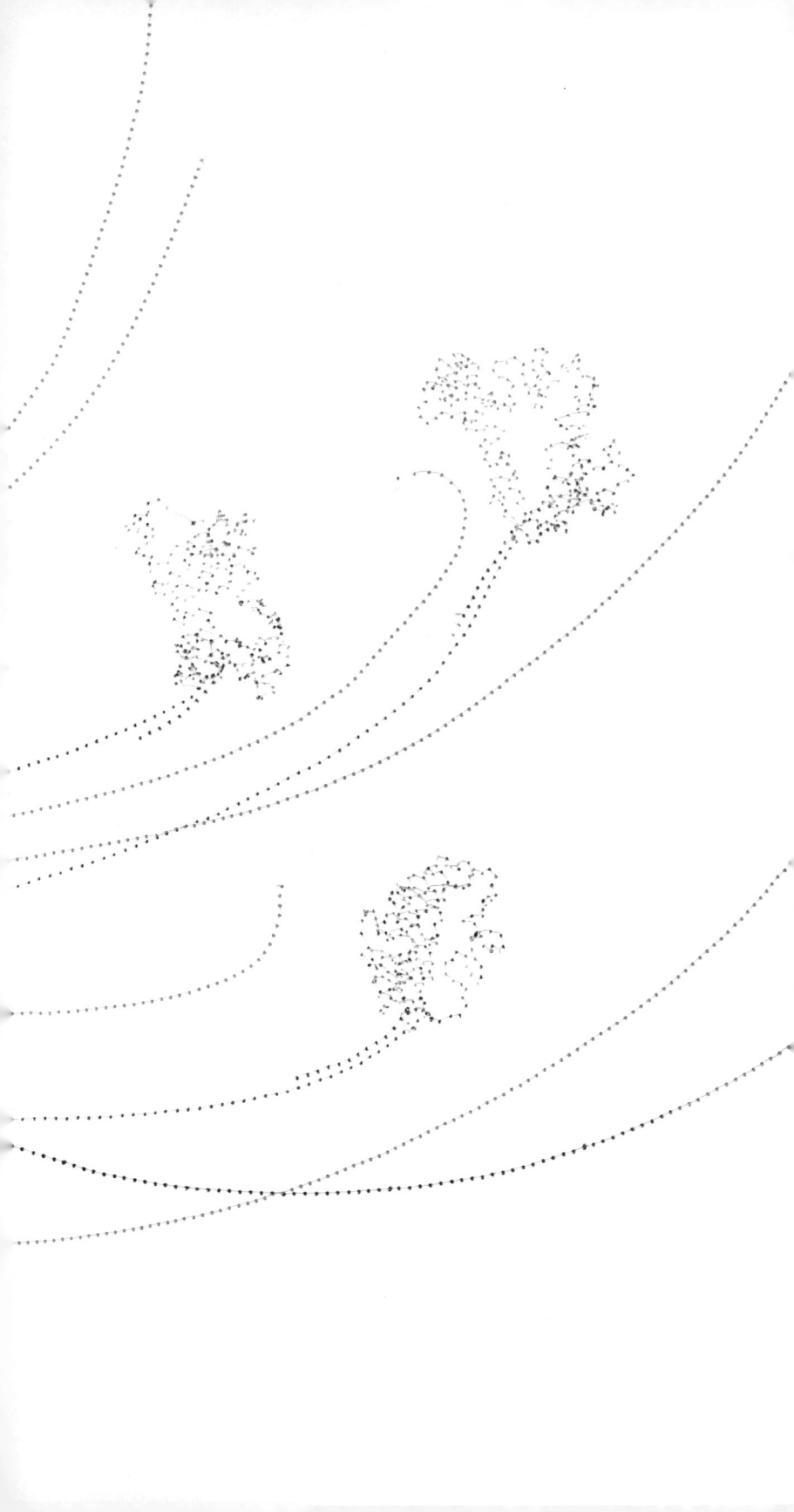

"It was after all
            "all Chintana had of
her. In fact it was all Belinda Kite had
"had of herself

                "—that once ago frail
embroidery her fingers had
                        "nimbly
and tenderly
            "stitched and bled upon,
finding in grassy thread the shape of

"a single

            "Harvester
                    "with dark orange
"wings,
            "long gone,

                        "yet by
which Chintana could now clearly
find,

        "recovering it,

            "reminding it,

                    "re-

"releasing it, as she had immediately
remembered when
                "Pravat had at last
handed it over to her

"—for this is what hurt so much—

"no deceit at all but the reach only of
                              "from
a longing and already
                    "parting
                              "woman.
 "A reach which tonight
                    "from this
same woman
              "had also saved five
children from the murder of
                              "fate.

   "And so Chintana tried hard to keep
breathing, even as her
                    "thumb throbbed
terribly and
              "a solitary tear
                              "sliced
down her cheek.

   "Which was when clock hands across
Upshur County finally
                    "clasped limply
around midnight and said goodbye.
Which was when
                    "Belinda Kite caught
sight of Chintana,
                    "coming apart,
"figuratively,
                    "with a tear that is,
                              "and
sneered—

   " 'Baby, your hubby was a lousy fuck.'

"From their window, the children were the first to see the snow
                         "splash
                                    "red.

    "Even before Belinda Kite
                              "knew what
was happening, before she could make
sense of the
                  "muffled screams and recoil
suddenly unrounding her as she,
                                  "right
on the spot,
              "literally,
                    "went to pieces.

"Tarff,

"Iniedia,

"Micit,

"Ezade and
"Sithiss

"saw all five
"fingers slide away
and tumble to the ground

"in a
soundless

"spray of blood.

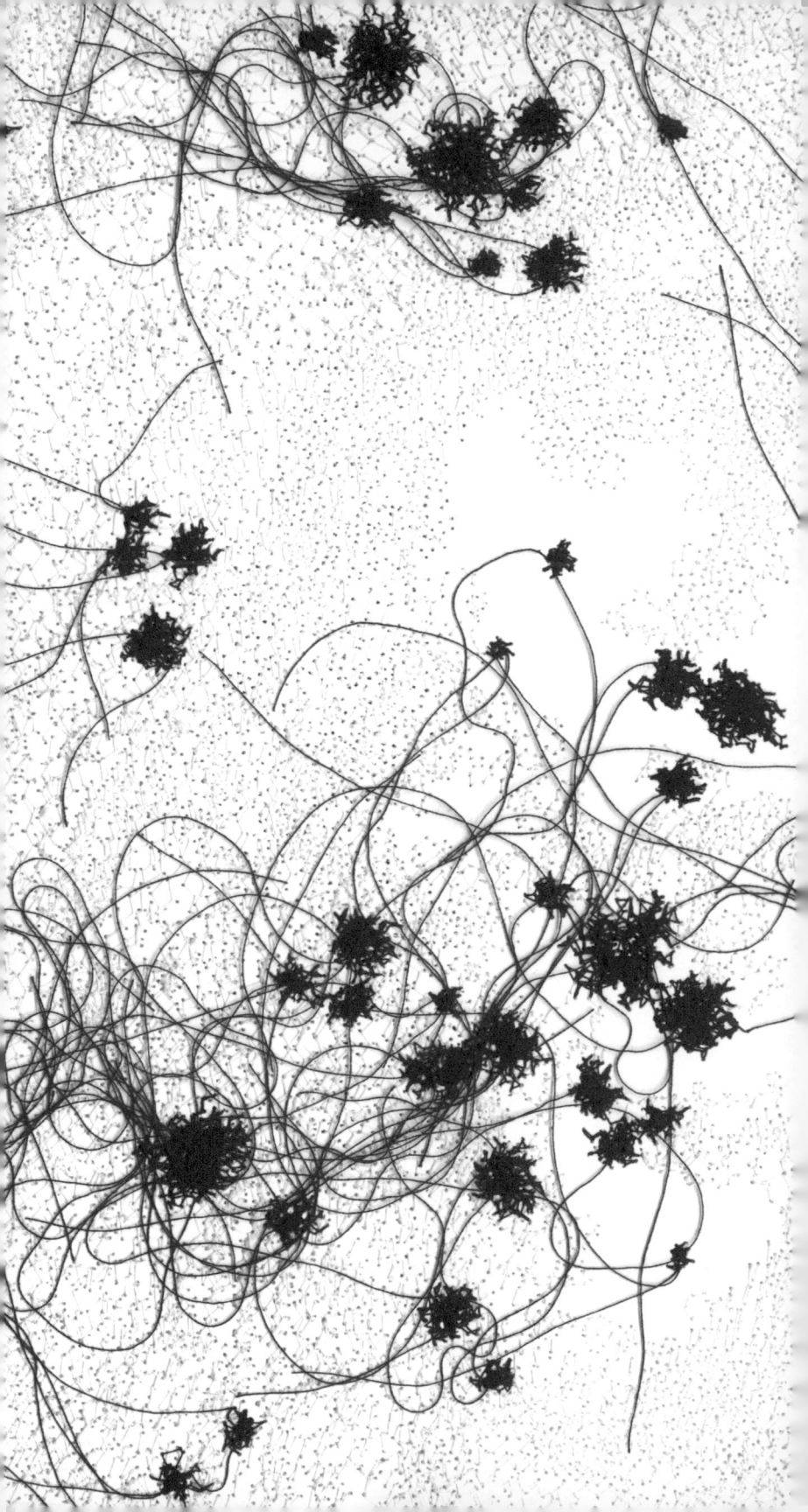

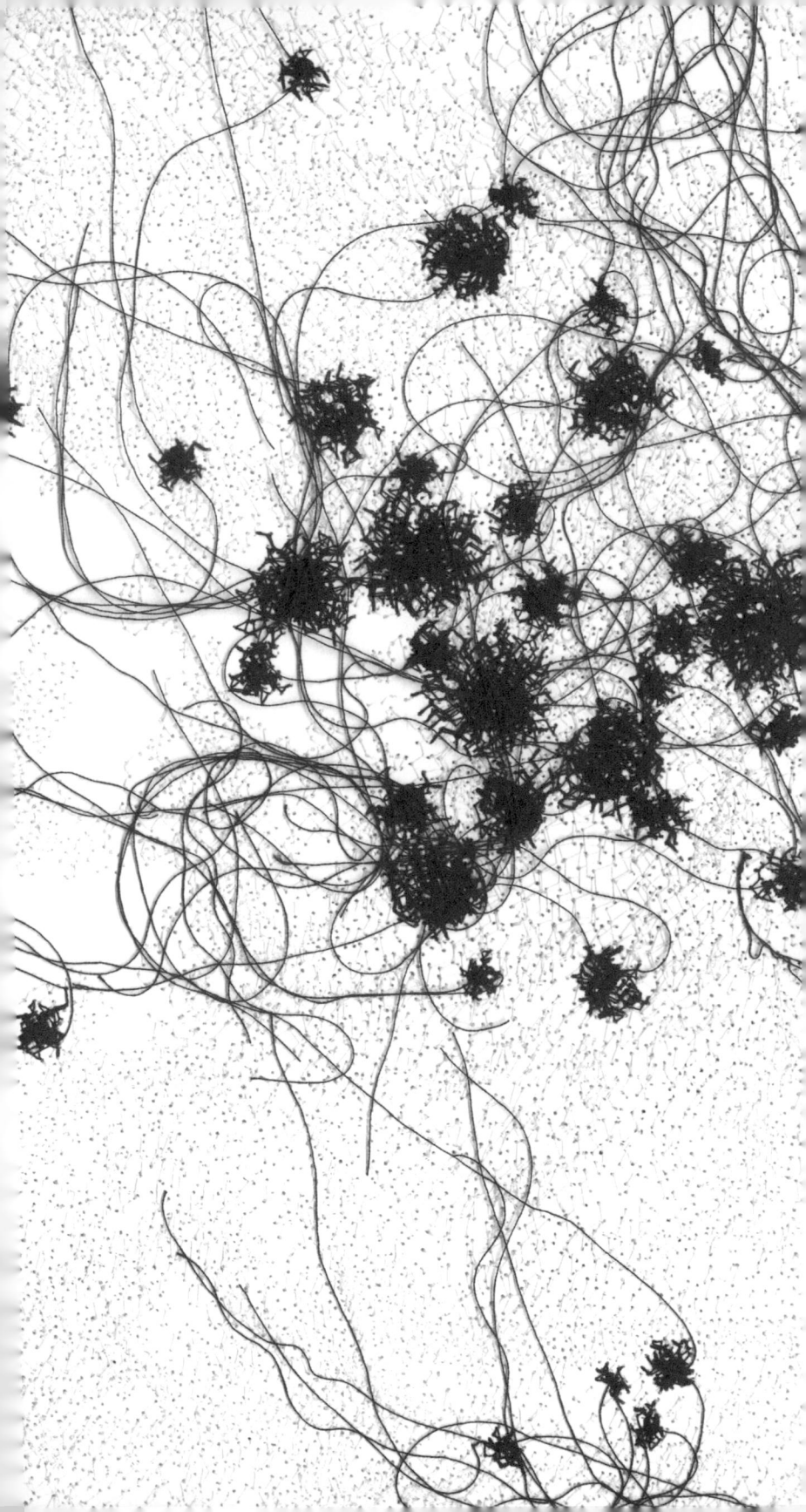

"But even as slices of joints and nails
scattered apart on the frosty stone,
                              "followed
by the slow tumbling
                    "slivers of the rest
of Belinda Kite's
              "hand,
                   "gold bangles
loose
      "too,
              "Chintana was already
"racing forward,
                    "direticating others
to call for help,
              "reaching—
                         "Oh
"how
                              "she reached for her!
      "—until
              "she was reaching
Belinda Kite
              "grabbing her
                         "holding her
"cradling her
              "in her arms,
                         "wrapping
her up tight in her grave coat,
                         "the scarf
tight around the tortured arm,
                         "stroking
the woman's head, which she understood
at any moment
              "could also fall
                         "away.

"And so
            "though Chantana kept
calling
            "aloud for someone,
                        "for anyone,
"inside she quietly continued to accept
the mercy laden
                        "merciless agony of what
"only survives as
                "entirely personal,
                            "without
"witness, all
            "that really matters here,
                            "hers,
"herself,
            "for now,
                    "holding onto it
"patiently
            "like she held onto,
                        "just as
she held onto,
            "Belinda Kite,
                        "gently and
painfully and
            "gratefully too,
                        "accepatating
them all,
            "and with great sloppy breaths
too,
        "even if she also continued to
wonder
            "just how long one such tiny
stitch of,
            "well you know,

"could really hold."

Stitching

by

ATELIER Z

{in alphabetical order}

Regina Gonzales

Claire Kohne

Michele Reverte

Special thanks to Tyler Martin, n8 rightmeier, and Peter van Sambeek for the ongoing inspirations of their talents and all the labor their dedication inspires. With additional thanks to VEM™ for Vocal Mesh & Identity Pattern Tracing. All I Take I Do All I Made I Lose All I Left I Let Another Take To Use . . .

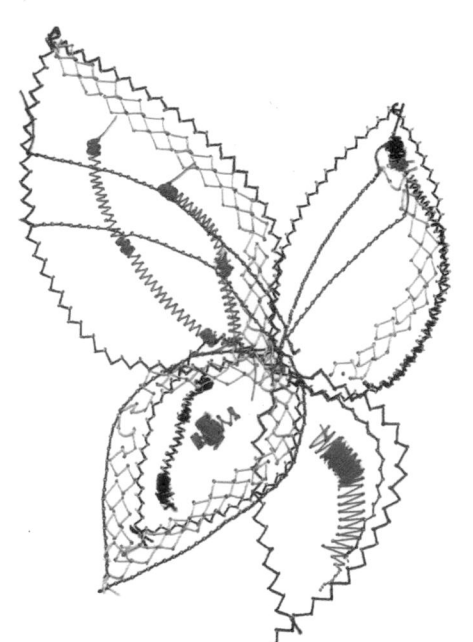

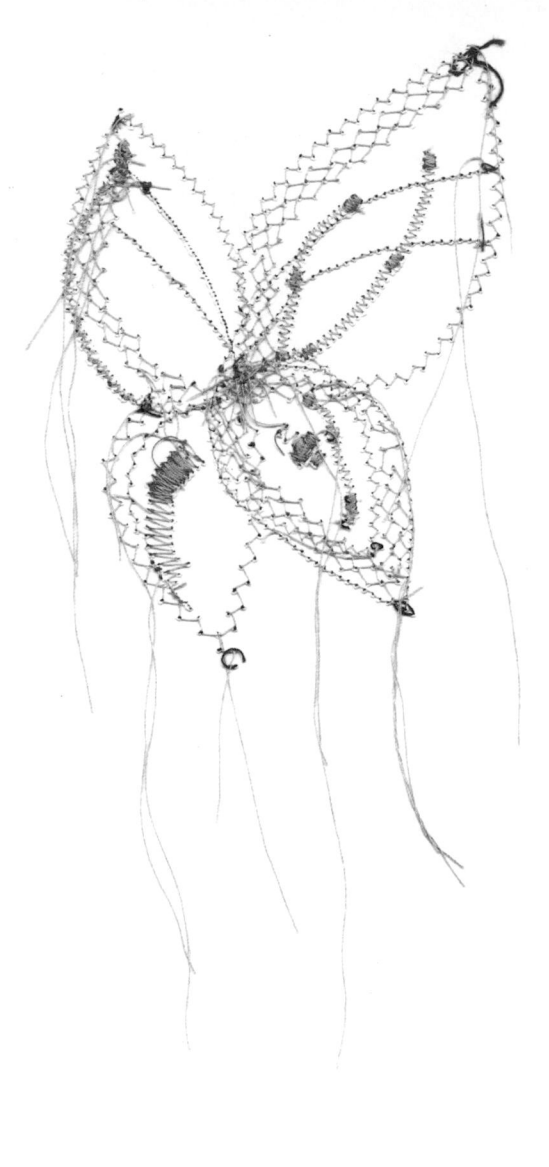

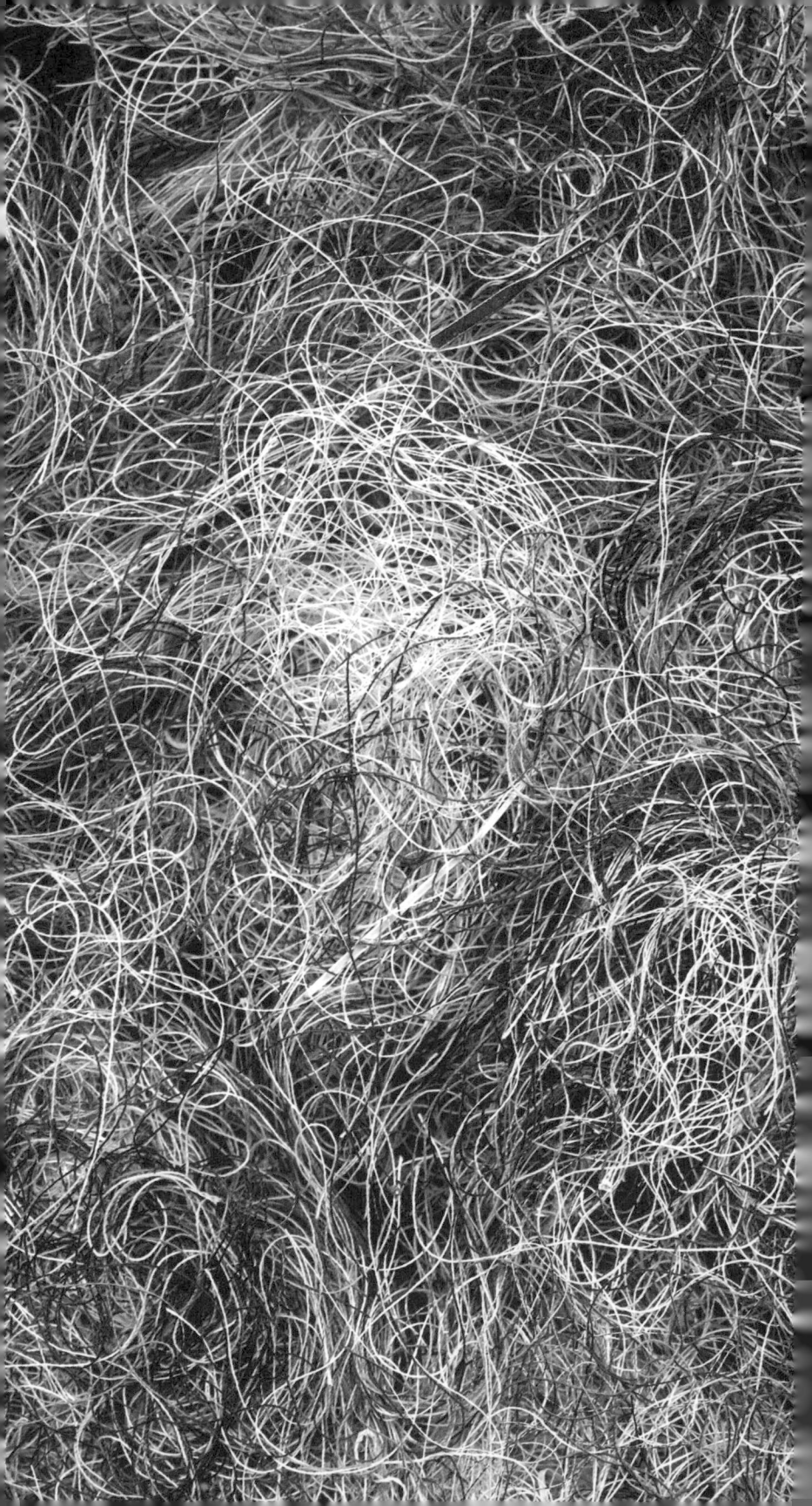